Curtiss Crane Gardiner

**The Papers and Biography of Lion Gardiner**

1599-1663

Curtiss Crane Gardiner

**The Papers and Biography of Lion Gardiner**
*1599-1663*

ISBN/EAN: 9783337074609

Printed in Europe, USA, Canada, Australia, Japan

Cover: Foto ©Raphael Reischuk / pixelio.de

More available books at **www.hansebooks.com**

# THE

# PAPERS AND BIOGRAPHY

OF

# LION GARDINER.

1599=1663.

## WITH AN APPENDIX.

Our ancestors, though not perfect and infallible in all respects, were a religious, brave and virtuous set of men, whose love of liberty, civil and religious, brought them from their native land into the American Deserts.
—Jonathan Mayhew, Election Sermon, 1754.

Edited, with Notes Critical and Illustrative,

BY

## CURTISS C. GARDINER.

ST. LOUIS:
PRINTED FOR THE EDITOR.
MDCCCLXXXIII.

PRESS OF
LEVISON & BLYTHE STATIONERY CO.,
ST. LOUIS.

# ANNOUNCEMENT.

I purpose to publish a volume, to be called the "Papers and Biography of Lion Gardiner." It will contain copies of his manuscripts, being reprints of manuscripts and autograph letters; gleanings from colonial histories and extracts from public and private records relating to events in which he bore a part. Also traditionary reminiscences and some account of his family name and arms. The whole to conclude with a biographical sketch and notes of reference.

I shall be able to show, from authentic sources, his nativity, early life and occupation; his departure from abroad and arrival in this country; his career in colonial times; his purchase and occupation of an island which bears his name; being the progenitor of a respectable family in America.

CURTISS C. GARDINER.

St. Louis, Missouri, July 14th, 1883.

# CONTENTS.

# PAPERS.

---

*Behind the documents there was a man.—Taine.*

# PAPERS.

## CHAPTER I.

### *WRITING IN A GENEVAN BIBLE.*

The writing on the fly-leaf of the Genevan Bible—*printed at London, 1599*—which is in the possession of the family at Gardiner's Island, has been pointed to for many generations as the hand-writing of Lion Gardiner; and until the discovery of his undoubted autograph letters it was not questioned.

This Genevan Bible was in the possession of the Conkling family of East Hampton, L. I., as late as the sixth generation from Lion Gardiner, when Elisha Conkling, a great-grandson of Lion Gardiner's daughter Mary, who married a Conkling, presented it to John Lyon Gardiner,(1) seventh proprietor of Gardiner's Island, since which time it has been counted among the valued relics of the family at the island.

The tradition is, that this bible was once the property of Lion Gardiner: yet it does not contain his name, nor any other name indicating ownership. The better opinion, as to the writing in this bible, seems to be that it is a copy of an original writing made by Lion Gardiner.

(1) John Lyon Gardiner was born at Gardiner's Island, November 8th, 1770. He was graduated at the College of New Jersey in the class of 1789. His father died while he was in his infancy, and the island was placed in the care of three trustees until he obtained his majority, when he became the seventh proprietor of the island. In 1798, he wrote a very interesting paper, entitled "Notes and Observations on the Town of East Hampton, L. I.," which included Gardiner's Island.—Vide Documentary History of N. Y., Vol. 1, p. 673, et seq. On March 4, 1803, he married Sarah Griswold of Lyme, Ct. The issue of this marriage was three sons and two daughters. He died November 22d, 1816. His widow survived him nearly fifty years. During the middle life of Mr. John Lyon Gardiner the Rev. Lyman Beecher was pastor of the church at East Hampton, L. I., from 1799 to 1809. We quote from Beecher's Autobiography—Vol. 1, p. 96. Referring to Gardiner's Island as being within his parish, he mentions the seventh of the series of owners as "a man of education and refinement, and celebrated for his fondness for antiquarian research. His society would naturally be attractive to a youthful minister, and accordingly the island, with its large and hospitable mansion, was ever one of his favorite visiting places; and during his East Hampton ministry, no sermon was ever thought ready for the press till it had been submitted to the inspection of his friend, John Lyon Gardiner."—C. C. G.

### COPY OF THE WRITING IN A GENEVAN BIBLE.

In the yeare of our Lord 1635, July the 10th, came I, Lion Gardiner and Mary my wife from Woerden, a towne in Holland, where my wife was borne, being the daughter of one Derike Wilamson, derocant; her mother's name was Hachini Bastians; her aunt, sister of her mother, was the wife of Wouter Leanderson, Old Burger Measter, dwelling in the bofaton over against the brossoen in the Unicorn's Head; her brother's name was Punc Gearstsen, Old Burger Measter. We came from Woerden to London, and from thence to New England, and dwelt at Saybrook forte four years, of which I was commander; and there was borne unto me a son named David, in 1636, April the 29, the first born in that place, and in 1638, a daughter was born to me called Mary, August the 30, and then I went to an island of mine owne, which I bought of the Indians, called by them Manchonoke, by us the Isle of Wite, and there was born another daughter named Elizabeth, Sept. the 14, 1641, she being the first child born theire of English parents.

The writing from which the above was copied is very irregular and considerably faded and defaced, and could hardly be deciphered by any one without some knowledge of the subject.

### COPY OF ANCIENT MANUSCRIPT.

The following is a copy of ancient manuscript, which, with the memorandum annexed to it, was copied from the records in the Family Bible of John Lyon Gardiner, seventh proprietor of Gardiner's Island: (1)

In the year of our Lord, 1635, the tenth of July, came I, Lion Gardiner and Mary my wife from Woerden a towne in Holland where my wife was born being the daughter of one Derike Wilemson deurcant; her mother's name was Hachin and her aunt, sister of her mother, was the wife of Wouter Leonardson old burger meester dwelling in the hostrate over against the Brewer in Unicorn's head; her brother's name was Punce Garretson also an old burgher meester. We came from Woerdon to London and from thence to New England and dwelt at Saybrooke fort four years, it is at the mouth of the Connecticut river, of which I was commander, and there was born to me a son named David, 1636, the 29th of April, the first born in that place, and 1638, a daughter was-born named Mary, the 30th of August, and then I went to an island of my owne which I had bought and purchased of the Indians, called by them Manchonake, by us the Isle of Weight, and there was born another daughter named Elizabeth the 14th of Sept., 1641, she being the first child of English parents that was born there.

MEMORANDUM BY JOHN LYON GARDINER, AUGUST 30TH, 1804.   *   *   *
The above writing is a literal copy of ancient manuscript in the possession of Miss Lucretia Gardiner, (2) daughter of David Gardiner of New London, from which it

(1) This family bible contains the births, marriages and deaths of the eldest sons, who had been proprietors of the island by entailment; but there is no information of the younger sons and daughters (?) The arrangement of all of the records is methodical and apparently complete, even to the minutest particulars. On the last printed page is the following: " This book was purchased, July 8th, anno domini 1803, by John Lyon Gardiner.—s, 3."—C. C. G.

(2) Miss Lucretia Gardiner was a daughter of David Gardiner who was a son of David Gardiner, fourth proprietor, and never married. What became of the ancient manuscript which was in her possession has not been ascertained. It appears there was another Miss Lucretia Gardiner, who never married, who was a daughter of John Gardiner, the only son of Jonathan Gardiner, one of the sons of John Gardiner, the third proprietor. The two Miss Lucretias were second cousins.—C. C. G.

is probable the writing in an old family bible, *printed at London*, 1599, was taken, as they are nearly similar, which bible was a few years since—about 1794—given to John L. Gardiner by Mr. Elisha Conkling of Wernot, being great-grandson of the above-mentioned Mary, who married Jeremiah Conkling of East Hampton, L. I., about 1658, and died June 15, 1727, aged 89.

The foregoing memorandum is a highly important paper. The character of its author at once stamps it as authentic. First, he states when and from whom he obtained the Genevan Bible at Gardiner's Island; second, he declares his "copy of ancient manuscript" to be "literal"; and adds, parenthetically; "*which*, it is probable, *the writing in an old family bible*," meaning the Genevan Bible, "*was taken*, as they are nearly similar." Accepting this statement as true, there can be no doubt but the writing in the Genevan Bible is a copy, and not an original record.

## CHAPTER II.

### *RELATION OF THE PEQUOT WARS.*

THE FOLLOWING "Letter" and "Relation of the Pequot Wars," by Lion Gardiner, are reprints copied verbatim et literatim from the Collections of the Massachusetts Historical Society, published in the year 1833, Vol. III, 3rd series, 131-160. The publishing committee state that "the original manuscript of this "Relation," and a copy in the handwriting of Gov. Jonathan Trumbull, the elder," were delivered to them for publication "by William T. Williams," a grandson of Gov. Trumbull, of Lebanon, Ct. The committee further state, "on account of the difficulty the printer would find in deciphering the original, have followed the orthography of the copy, excepting in the proper names, where they thought it of more importance to adhere to the ancient orthography." The existence of this manuscript was known to historical writers many years before it was published. It is said to have formerly belonged to the Winthrop family of New London. B. Trumbull's His. of Conn., 2 vols., New Haven, 1797 and 1818, refers to "Manuscripts of Gardiner," Vol. I, 61; but whether the manuscript has been preserved, to the present time, cannot be ascertained. Neither of the historical societies of New England have the custody of it. In accordance with the custom of historical societies the manuscript is printed without making corrections; even the name Gardiner is printed Gardener because, it may be, the letter intended for an i, does not happen to be dotted, obviously the result of carelessness. The subject matter is both spirited and entertaining; the style is stately and quaint, frequently amusing and always exact, and abounds in scriptural phrases after the manner of the Puritans.

The reader will bear in mind that this is a copy of original manuscript written in the seventeenth century, by an aged man, **who had dwelt** twenty-five years in a wilderness; yet Lion Gardiner's orthography, as well as phraseology, will compare favorably with the best specimens of his distinguished contemporaries.

### LETTER.

### EAST HAMPTON, *June 12, 1660.*

Loving Friends. Robert Chapman and Thomas Hurlburt: My love remembered to you both, these are to inform, that as you desired me when I was with you and Major Mason at Seabrooke two years and a half ago to consider and call to mind the passages of God's Providence at Seabrooke in and about the time of the Pequit War, wherein I have now endeavoured to answer your desires and having rummaged and found some old papers then written it was a great help to my memory. You know that when I came to you I was an engineer or architect, whereof carpentry is a little part, but you know I could never use all the tools, for although for my necessity, I was forced sometimes to use my shifting chissel, and my holdfast, yet you know I could never endure nor abide the smoothing plane; I have sent you a piece of timber scored and forehewed unfit to join to any handsome piece of work, but seeing I have done the hardest work, you must get somebody to chip it and to smooth it lest the splinters should prick some men's fingers, for the truth must not be spoken at all times, though to my knowledge I have written nothing but the truth, and you may take out or put in what you please, or if you will, throw it all into the fire; but I think you may let the Governor and Major Mason see it. I have also inserted some additions of things that were done since, that they may be considered together. And thus as I was when I was with you, so I remain still.

Your Loving Friend,

LION GARDINER.

### RELATION.

In the year 1635, I, Lion Gardiner, engineer and master of works of fortification in the legers of the Prince of Orange, in the Low Countries, through the persuasion of Mr. John Davenport, Mr. Hugh Peters with some other well-affected Englishmen of Rotterdam, I made an agreement with the forenamed Mr. Peters for £100 per annum, for four years, to serve the company of patentees, namely, the Lord Say, the Lord Brooks, Sir Arthur Hazilrig, Sir Mathew Bonnington, Sir Richard Saltingstone, Esquire Fenwick, and the rest of their company. I was to serve them only in the drawing, ordering and making of a city, towns or forts of defence.

And so I came from Holland to London, and from thence to New England, where I was appointed to attend such orders as Mr. John Winthrop, Esquire, the present Governor of Conectecott, was to appoint, whether at Pequit river, or Conectecott, and that we should choose a place both for the convenience of a good harbour, and also for capableness and fitness for fortification.

But I landing at Boston the latter end of November, the aforesaid Mr. Winthrop had sent before one Lieut. Gibbons, Sergeant Willard, with some carpenters, to take possession of the river's mouth, where they began to build houses against the spring; we expecting, according to promise, that there would have come from England to us 300 able men, whereof 200 should attend fortification, 50 to till the ground, and 50 to build houses.

But our great expectation at the river's mouth came only to two

men, viz. Mr. Fenwick, and his man, who came with Mr. Hugh Peters,
and Mr. Oldham and Thomas Stanton, bringing with them some
otter-skin coats, and beaver, and skeins of wampum, which the Pequits had sent for a present, because the English had required those
Pequits that had killed a Virginean, one Capt. Stone, with his bark's
crew, in Conectecott river, for they said they would have their lives
and not their presents; then I answered, "seeing you will take Mr.
Winthrop to the Bay to see his wife, newly brought to bed of her
first child, and though you say he shall return, yet I know if you
make war with these Pequits, he will not come hither again, for I
know you will keep yourselves safe, as you think, in the Bay, but
myself, with these few, you will leave at the stake to be roasted, or
for hunger to be starved, for Indian corn is now 12s. per bushel, and
we have but three acres planted, and if they will now make war for
a Virginian and expose us to the Indians, whose mercies are cruel-
ties, they, I say, love the Virginians better than us: for, have they
stayed these four or five years, and will they begin now, we being so
few in the river, and have scarce holes to put our heads in?"

I pray ask the Magistrates in the Bay if they have forgot what
I said to them when they returned from Salem? For Mr. Winthrop,
Mr. Haines, Mr. Dudley, Mr. Ludlow, Mr. Humfry, Mr. Belingam, Mr.
Coddington, and Mr. Nowell;—these entreated me to go with Mr.
Humfry and Mr. Peters to view the country, to see how fit it was for
fortification. And I told them that nature had done more than half
the work already, and I thought no foreign potent enemy would do
them any hurt, but one that was near. They asked me who that was,
and I said it was Capt. Hunger that threatened them most, for, said
I, "war is like a three-footed stool, want one foot and down comes
all; and these three feet are men, victuals, and munition, therefore,
seeing in peace you are like to be famished, what will or can be
done if war? Therefore I think," said I, "it will be best only to
fight against Capt. Hunger, and let fortification alone awhile; and if
need hereafter require it, I can come to do you any service:" and
they all liked my saying well.

Entreat them to rest awhile, till we get more strength here about
us, and that we hear where the seat of war will be, may approve of
it, and provide for it, for I had but twenty-four in all, men, women,

and boys and girls, and not food for them for two months, unless we saved our corn-field, which could not possibly be if they came to war, for it is two miles from our home.

Mr. Winthrop, Mr. Fenwick, and Mr. Peters promised me that they would do their utmost endeavour to persuade the Bay-men to desist from war a year or two, till we could be better provided for it; and then the Pequit Sachem was sent for, and the present returned, but full sore against my will.

So they three returned to Boston, and two or three days after came an Indian from Pequit, whose name was Cocommithus, who had lived at Plimoth, and could speak good English; he desired that Mr. Steven Winthrop go to Pequit with an £100 worth of trucking cioth and all other trading ware, for they knew that we had a great cargo of goods of Mr. Pincheon's, and Mr. Steven Winthrop had the disposing of it. And he said that if he would come he might put off all his goods, and the Pequit Sachem would give him two horses that had been there a great while. So I sent the shallop with Mr. Steven Winthrop, Sergeant Tille, whom we called afterward Sergeant Kettle, because he put the kettle on his head, and Thomas Hurlbut and three men more, charging them that they should ride in the middle of the river, and not go ashore until they had done all their trade, and that Mr. Steven Winthrop should stand in the hold of the boat, having their guns by them, and swords by their sides, the other four to be, two in the fore cuddie, and two in aft, being armed in like manner, that so they out of the loop-holes might clear the boat, if they were by the Pequits assaulted; and that they should let but one canoe come aboard at once, with no more but four Indians in her, and when she had traded then another, and that they should lie no longer there than one day, and at night to go out of the river; and if they brought the two horses, to take them in a clear piece of land at the mouth of the river, two of them to go ashore to help the horses in, and the rest stand ready with their guns in their hands, if need were, to defend them from the Pequits, for I durst not trust them. So they went and found but little trade, and they having forgotten what I charged them, Thomas Hurlbut and one more went ashore to boil the kettle, and Thomas Hurlbut stepping into the Sachem's wigwam, not far from the shore, enquiring for the horses, the Indians

went out of the wigwam, and Wincumbone, his mother's sister, was
then the great Pequit Sachem's wife, who made signs to him that he
should be gone, for they would cut off his head; which, when he per-
ceived, he drew his sword and ran to the others, and got aboard, and
immediately came abundance of Indians to the water-side and called
them to come ashore, but they immediately set sail and came home,
and this caused me to keep watch and ward, for I saw they plotted
our destruction.

And suddenly after came Capt. Endecott, Capt. Turner, and Capt.
Undrill, with a company of soldiers, well fitted, to Seabrook, and
made that place their rendezvous or seat of war, and that to my great
grief, for, said I, "you come hither to raise these wasps about my
ears, and then you will take wing and flee away;" but when I had
seen their commission I wondered, and made many allegations
against the manner of it, but go they did to Pequit, and as they
came without acquainting any of us in the river with it, so they went
against our will, for I knew that I should loose our corn-field; then
I entreated them to hear what I would say to them, which was this:
"sirs, seeing you will go, I pray you, if you don't load your barks
with Pequits, load them with corn, for that is now gathered with
them, and dry, ready to put into their barns, and both you and we
have need of it, and I will send my shallop and hire this Dutchman's
boat, there present, to go with you, and if you cannot attain your
end of the Pequits, yet you may load your barks with corn, which
will be welcome to Boston and to me;" But they said they had no
bags to load them with, then said I, "here is three dozen of new bags,
you shall have thirty of them, and my shallop to carry them, and six
of them my men shall use themselves, for I will with the Dutchmen
send twelve men well provided;" and I desired them to divide the
men into three parts, viz. two parts to stand without the corn, and to
defend the other one-third part, that carried the corn to the water-
side, till they have loaded what they can. And the men there in
arms, when the rest are aboard, shall in order go aboard, the rest
that are aboard shall with their arms clear the shore, if the Pequits
do assault them in the rear, and then, when the General shall display
his colours, all to set sail together. To this motion they all agreed,
and I put the three dozen of bags aboard my shallop, and away they

went, and demanded the Pequit Sachem to come into parley. But it was returned for answer, that he was from home, but within three hours he would come; and so from three to six, and thence to nine, there came none. But the Indians came without arms to our men, in great numbers, and they talked with my men, whom they knew; but in the end, at a word given, they all on a sudden ran away from our men, as they stood in rank and file, and not an Indian more was to be seen: and all this while before, they carried all their stuff away, and thus was that great parley ended. Then they displayed their colours, and beat their drums, burnt' some wigwams and some heaps of corn, and my men carried as much aboard as they could, but the army went aboard, leaving my men ashore, which ought to have marched aboard first. But they all set sail, and my men were pursued by the Indians, and they hurt some of the Indians, two of them came home wounded. The Bay-men killed not a man, save that one Kichomiquim, an Indian Sachem of the Bay, killed a Pequit; and thus began the war between the Indians and us in these parts.

So my men being come home, and having brought a pretty quantity of corn with them, they informed me, both Dutch and English, of all passages. I was glad of the corn.

After this I immediately took men and went to our corn-field, to gather our corn, appointing others to come about with the shallop and fetch it, and left five lusty men in the strong-house, with long guns, which house I had built for the defence of the corn. Now these men not regarding the charge I had given them, three of them went a mile from the house a fowling; and having loaded themselves with fowl they returned. But the Pequits let them pass first, till they had loaded themselves, but at their return they arose out of their ambush, and shot them all three; one of them escaped through the corn, shot through the leg, the other two they tormented. Then the next day I sent the shallop to fetch the five men, and the rest of the corn that was broken down, and they found but three, as is above said, and when they had gotten that they left the rest; and as soon as they had gone a little way from shore they saw the house on fire.

Now so soon as the boat came home, and brought us this bad

news, old Mr. Michell was very urgent with me to lend him the boat to fetch hay home from the Six-mile Island, but I told him they were too few men, for his four men could but carry the hay aboard, and one must stand in the boat to defend them, and they must have two more at the foot of the Rock, with their guns, to keep the Indians from running down upon them. And in the first place, before they carry any of the cocks of hay, to scour the meadow with their three dogs,—to march all abreast from the lower end up to the Rock, and if they found the meadow clear, then to load their hay; but this was also neglected, for they all went ashore and fell to carrying off their hay, and the Indians presently rose out of the long grass, and killed three, and took the brother of Mr. Michell, who is the minister of Cambridge, and roasted him alive; and so they served a shallop of his, coming down the river in the Spring, having two men, one whereof they killed at Six-mile Island, the other came down drowned to us ashore at our doors, with an arrow shot into his eye through his head.

In the 22d of February, I went out with ten men and three dogs, half a mile from the house, to burn the weeds, leaves and reeds, upon the neck of land, because we had felled twenty timber-trees, which we were to roll to the water-side to bring home, every man carrying a length of match with brimstone-matches with him to kindle the fire withal. But when we came to the small of the Neck, the weeds burning, I having before this set two sentinels on the small of the Neck, I called to the men that were burning the reeds to come away, but they would not until they had burnt up the rest of their matches. Presently there starts up four Indians out of the fiery reeds, but ran away, I calling to the rest of our men to come away out of the marsh. Then Robert Chapman and Thomas Hurlbut, being sentinels, called to me, saying there came a number of Indians out of the other side of the marsh. Then I went to stop them, that they should not get the wood-land; but Thomas Hurlbut cried out to me that some of the men did not follow me, for Thomas Rumble and Arthur Branch, threw down their two guns and ran away; then the Indians shot two of them that were in the reeds, and sought to get between us and home, but durst not come before us, but kept us in a half-moon, we retreating and exchanging many a

shot, so that Thomas Hurlbut was shot almost through the thigh,
John Spencer in the back, into his kidneys, myself into the thigh,
two more were shot dead. But in our retreat I kept Hurlbut and
Spencer still before us, we defending ourselves with our naked
swords, or else they had taken us all alive, so that the two sore
wounded men, by our slow retreat, got home with their guns, when
our two sound men ran away and left their guns behind them. But
when I saw the cowards that left us, I resolved to let them draw lots
which of them should be hanged, for the articles did hang up in
the hall for them to read, and they knew they had been published long before. But at the intercession of old Mr. Michell, Mr.
Higgisson, and Mr. Pell, I did forbear.

Within a few days after, when I had cured myself of my wound,
I went out with eight men to get some fowl for our relief, and found
the guns that were thrown away, and the body of one man shot
through, the arrow going in at the right side, the head sticking fast,
half through a rib on the left side, which I took out and cleansed it,
and presumed to send to the Bay, because they had said that the
arrows of the Indians were of no force.

Anthony Dike, master of a bark, having his bark at Rhode
Island in the winter, was sent by Mr. Vane, then Governor.
Anthony came to Rhode Island by land, and from thence he came
with his bark to me with a letter, wherein was desired that I
should consider and prescribe the best way I could to quell these
Pequits, which I also did, and with my letter sent the man's rib
as a token.

A few days after came Thomas Stanton down the river, and
staying for a wind, while he was there came a troop of Indians
within musket shot, laying themselves and their arms down behind
a little rising hill and two great trees; which I perceiving, called
the carpenter whom I had shewed how to charge and level a gun,
and that he should put two cartridges of musket bullets into two
sakers guns that lay about; and we levelled them against the place,
and I told him that he must look towards me, and when he saw me
wave my hat above my head he should give fire to both the guns;
then presently came three Indians, creeping out and calling to us to
speak with us; and I was glad that Thomas Stanton was there, and

I sent six men down by the Garden Pales to look that none should come under the hill behind us; and having placed the rest in places convenient closely, Thomas and I with my sword, pistol and carbine, went ten or twelve poles without the gate to parley with them. And when the six men came to the Garden Pales, at the corner, they found a great number of Indians creeping behind the fort, or betwixt us and home, but they ran away. Now I had said to Thomas Stanton, whatsoever they say to you, tell me first, for we will not answer them directly to anything, for I know not the mind of the rest of the English. So they came forth, calling us nearer to them, and we them nearer to us. But I would not let Thomas go any further than the great stump of a tree, and I stood by him; then they asked who we were, and he answered "Thomas and Lieutenant." But they said he lied, for I was shot with many arrows; and so I was, but my buff coat preserved me, only one hurt me. But when I spake to them they knew my voice, for one of them had dwelt three months with us, but ran away when the Bay-men came first. Then they asked us if we would fight with Niantecut Indians, for they were our friends and came to trade with us. We said we knew not the Indians one from another, and therefore would trade with none. Then they said, have you fought enough? We said we knew not yet. Then they asked if we did use to kill women and children? We said that they should see that hereafter. So they were silent a small space, and then they said, We are Pequits, and have killed Englishmen, and can kill them as mosquetoes, and we will go to Conectecott and kill men, women, and children, and we will take away the horses, cows and hogs. When Thomas Stanton had told me this, he prayed me to shoot that rogue, for, said he, he hath an Englishman's coat on, and saith that he hath killed three, and these other four have their cloathes on their backs. I said, "no, it is not the manner of a parley, but have patience and I shall fit them ere they go." "Nay, now or never," said he; so when he could get no other answer but this last, I bid him tell them that they should not go to Conectecott, for if they did kill all the men, and take all the rest as they said, it would do them no good, but hurt, for Englishwomen are lazy, and can't do their work; horses and cows will spoil your corn-fields, and the hogs their clam-banks, and so undo them : then I pointed to our great house, and bid him tell them there lay twenty pieces of trucking cloth, of Mr. Pincheon's, with hoes, hatchets, and all manner of trade, they were better fight still with us, and so get all that, and then go up the river after they had killed all us. Having heard this, they were mad as dogs, and ran away; then when they came to the place from whence they came, I waved my hat about my head, and the two great guns went off, so that there was a great hubbub amongst them.

Then two days after came down Capt. Mason, and Sergeant Seely, with five men more, to see how it was with us; and whilst they were there, came down a Dutch boat, telling us the Indians had killed fourteen English, for by that boat I had sent up letters to Conectecott, what I heard, and what I thought, and how to prevent that threatened danger, and received back again rather a scoff, than any thanks for my care and pains. But as I wrote, so it fell out to my great grief and theirs, for the next, or second day after, as Major Mason well knows, came down a great many canoes, going down the creek beyond the marsh, before the fort, many of them having white shirts; then I commanded the carpenter whom I had shewed to level great guns, to put in two round shot in the two sackers, and we levelled them at a certain place, and I stood to bid him give fire, when I thought the canoe would meet the bullet, and one of them took off the nose of a great canoe wherein the two maids were, that were taken by the Indians, whom I redeemed and clothed, for the Dutchmen, whom I sent to fetch them, brought them away almost naked from Pequit, they putting on their own linen jackets to cover their nakedness; and though the redemption cost me ten pounds, I am yet to have thanks for my care and charge about them: these things are known to Major Mason.

Then came from the Bay Mr. Tille, with a permit to go up to Harford, and coming ashore he saw a paper nailed up over the gate, whereon was written that no boat or bark should pass the fort, but that they come to an anchor first, that I might see whether they were armed and manned sufficiently, and they were not to land any where after they passed the fort till they came to Wethersfield; and this I did because Mr. Michell had lost a shallop before coming down from Wethersfield, with three men well armed. This Mr. Tille

gave me ill language for my presumption, as he called it, with other
expressions too long here to write.    When he had done I bid him go
to his warehouse, which he had built before I came, to fetch his
goods from thence, for I would watch no longer over it.   So he, knowing nothing, went and found his house burnt, and one of Mr. Plum's
with others, and he told me to my face that I had caused it to be
done ; but Mr. Higgisson, Mr. Pell, Mr. Thomas Hurlbut and John
Green can witness that the same day that our house was burnt at
Cornfield-point I went with Mr. Higgisson, Mr. Pell, and four men
more, broke open a door and took a note of all that was in the house
and gave it to Mr. Higgisson to keep, and so brought all the goods
to our house, and delivered it all to them again when they came for
it, without any penny of charge.   Now the very next day after I had
taken the goods out, before the sun was quite down, and we all together in the great hall, all them houses were on fire in one instant.
The Indians ran away, but I would not follow them.   Now when Mr.
Tille had received all his goods I said unto him, I thought I had
deserved for my honest care both for their bodies and goods of those
that passed by here, at the least better language, and am resolved to
order such maleperl persons as you are; therefore I wish you and
also charge you to observe that which you have read at the gate, 'tis
my duty to God, my masters, and my love I bear to you all which is
the ground of this, had you but eyes to see it ; but you will not till
you feel it.   So he went up the river, and when he came down again
to his place, which I call Tille's folly, now called Tille's point, in our
sight in despite, having a fair wind he came to an anchor, and with
one man more went ashore, discharged his gun, and the Indians fell
upon him, and killed the other, and carried him alive over the river
in our sight, before my shallop could come to them ; for immediately I sent seven men to fetch the Pink down, or else it had been
taken and three men more.   So they brought her down, and I sent
Mr. Higgisson and Mr. Pell aboard to take an invoice of all that was
in the vessel, that nothing might be lost.

    Two days after came to me, as I had written to Sir Henerie Vane,
then Governor of the Bay, I say came to me Capt. Undrill, with twenty
lusty men, well armed, to stay with me two months, or 'till something should be done about the Pequits.   He came at the charge of
my masters.

Soon after came down from Harford Maj. Mason, Lieut. Seely, accompanied with Mr. Stone and eighty Englishmen, and eighty Indians, with a commission from Mr. Ludlow and Mr. Steel, and some others; these came to go fight with the Pequits. But when Capt Undrill and I had seen their commission, we both said they were not fitted for such a design, and we said to Maj. Mason, we wondered he would venture himself, being no better fitted; and he said the Magistrates could not or would not send better: then we said that none of our men should go with them, neither should they go unless we, that were bred soldiers from our youth, could see some likelihood to do better than the Bay-men with their strong commission last year.

Then I asked them how they durst trust the Mohegin Indians, who had but that year come from the Pequits. They said they would trust them, for they could not well go without them for want of guides. Yea, said I, but I will try them before a man of ours shall go with you or them; and I called for Uncas and said unto him, " you say you will help Maj. Mason, but I will first see it, therefore send you now twenty men to the Bass river, for there went yesternight six Indians in a canoe thither; fetch them now dead or alive, and then you shall go with Maj. Mason, else not." So he sent his men who killed four, brought one a traitor to us alive, whose name was Kiswas, and one run away. And I gave him fifteen yards of trading cloth on my own charge, to give unto his men according to their desert. And having staid there five or six days before we could agree, at last we old soldiers agreed about the way and act, and took twenty insufficient men from the eighty that came from Harford and sent them up again in a shallop, and Capt. Undrill with twenty of the lustiest of our men went in their room, and I furnished them with such things as they wanted, and sent Mr. Pell, the surgeon with them; and the Lord God blessed their design and way, so that they returned with victory to the glory of God, and honour of our nation, having slain three hundred, burnt their fort, and taken many prisoners.

Then came to me an Indian called Wequash, and I by Mr. Higgisson inquired of him, how many of the Pequits were yet alive that had helped to kill Englishmen; and he declared them to Mr. Higgisson, and he writ them down, as may appear by his own hand here enclosed, and I did as therein is written.

Then three days after the fight came Waiandance, next brother to the old Sachem of Long Island, and having been recommended to me by Maj. Gibbons, he came to know if we were angry with all Indians. I answered "no, but only with such as had killed Englishmen." He asked me whether they that lived upon Long Island might come to trade with us? I said "no, nor we with them, for if I should send my boat to trade for corn, and you have Pequits with you, and if my boat should come into some creek by reason of bad weather, they might kill my men, and I shall think that you of Long-Island have done it, and so we may kill all you for the Pequits; but if you will kill all the Pequits that come to you, and send me their heads, then I will give to you as to Weakwash, and you shall have trade with us." Then, said he, I will go to my brother, for he is the great Sachem of Long-Island, and if we may have peace and trade with you, we will give you tribute as we did the Pequits. Then I said, "If you have any Indians that have killed English, you must bring their heads also." He answered not any one, and said that Gibbons, my brother would have told you if it had been so; so he went away and did as I had said, and sent me five heads, three and four heads for which I paid them that brought them as I had promised.

Then came Capt. Stoten with an army of 300 men, from the Bay, to kill the Pequits; but they were fled beyond New Haven to a swamp. I sent Wequash after them, who went by night to spy them out, and the army followed him, and found them at the great swamp, who killed some and took others, and the rest fled to the Mowhakues with their Sachem. Then the Mohaws cut off his head and sent it to Harford, for then they all feared us, but now it is otherwise, for they say to our faces that our Commissioner's meeting once a year, and speak a great deal, or write a letter, and there's all for they dare not fight. But before they went to the Great Swamp they sent Thomas Stanton over to Long Island and Shelter Island, to find Pequits there, but there was none, for the Sachem Waiandance, that, was at Plimoth when the Commissioners were there, and set there last, I say, he had killed so many of the Pequits, and sent their heads to me, that they durst not come there; and he and his men went with the English to the Swamp, and thus the Pequits were quelled at that time.

But there was like to be a great broil between Miantenomie and Unchus who should have the rest of the Pequits, but we mediated between them and pacified them; also Unchus challenged the Narraganset Sachem out to a single combat, but he would not fight without all his men; but they were pacified, though the old grudge remained still, as it doth appear.

Thus far I had written in a book, that all men and posterity might know how and why so many honest men had their blood shed, yea, and some flayed alive, others cut in pieces, and some roasted alive, only because Kichamokin, a Bay Indian killed one Pequit; and thus far of the Pequit war, which was but a comedy in comparison of the tragedies which hath been here threatened since, and may yet come, if God do not open the eyes, ears, and hearts of some that I think are wilfully deaf and blind, and think because there is no change that the vision fails, and put the evil threatened-day far off, for say they, we are now twenty to one to what we were then, and none dare meddle with us. Oh! wo be to the pride and security which hath been the ruin of many nations, as woful experience has proved.

But I wonder, and so doth many more with me, that the Bay doth not better revenge the murdering of Mr. Oldham, an honest man of their own, seeing they were at such cost for a Virginian. The Narragansets that were at Block-Island killed him, and had £50 of gold of his, for I saw it when he had five pieces of me, and put it up into a clout and tied it up altogether, when he went away from me to Block-Island; but the Narragansets had it and punched holes into it, and put it about their necks for jewels: and afterwards I saw the Dutch have some of it, which they had of the Narragansets at a small rate.

And now I find that to be true which our friend Waiandance told me many years ago, and that was this; that seeing all the plots of the Narragansets were always discovered, he said they would let us alone till they had destroyed Uncas, and him, and then they, with the Mowquakes and Mowhaukes and the Indians beyond the Dutch, and all the Northern and Eastern Indians, would easily destroy us, man and mother's son. This have I informed the Governors of these parts, but all in vain, for I see they have done as those of Wethersfield, not regarding till they were impelled to it by blood; and thus we may be sure of the fattest of the flock are like to go first, if not altogether, and then it will be too late to read Jer. xxv.—for drink we shall if the Lord be not the more merciful to us for our extreme pride and base security, which cannot but stink before the Lord; and we may expect this, that if there should be war again between England and Holland, our friends at the Dutch and our Dutch Englishmen would prove as true to us now, as they were when the fleet came out of England; but no more of that, a word to the wise is enough.

And now I am old, I would fain die a natural death, or like a soldier in the field, with honor, and not to have a sharp stake set in the ground, and thrust into my fundament, and to have my skin flayed off by piece-meal, and cut in pieces and bits, and my flesh roasted and thrust down my throat, as these people have done, and I know will be done to the chiefest in the country by hundreds, if God should deliver us into their hands, as justly he may for our sins.

I going over to Meantecut, upon the eastern end of Long Island, upon some occasion that I had there, I found four Narragansets there talking with the Sachem and his old counsellors. I asked an Indian what they were? He said that they were Narragansets, and that one was Miannemo, a Sachem. "What came they for?".said I. He said he knew not, for they talked secretly; so I departed to another wigwam. Shortly after came the Sachem Waiandance to me and said, do you know what these came for? "No," said I; then he said, they say I must give no more wampum to the English, for they are no Sachems, nor none of their children shall be in their place if they die; and they have no tribute given them; there is but one king in England, who is over them all, and if you would send him 100,000 fathom of wampum, he would not give you a knife for it, nor thank you. And I said to them, Then they will come and kill us all, as they did the Pequits; then they said, no, the Pequits gave them wampum and beaver, which they loved so well, but they sent it them again, and killed them because they had killed an Englishman; but you have killed none, therefore give them nothing. Now friend, tell me what I shall say to them, for one of them is a great man. Then said I, "tell them that you must go first to the farther end of Long-Island, and speak with all the rest, and a month hence you will give them an answer. Mean time you may go to Mr. Haines, and he will tell you what to do, and I will write all this now in my book that I have here:" and so he did, and the Narragansets departed, and this Sachem came to me at my house, and I wrote this matter to Mr. Haines, and he went up with Mr. Haines, who forbid him to give anything to the Narraganset, and writ to me so.—And when they came again they came by my Island, and I knew them to be the same men; and I told them they might go home again, and I gave them Mr. Haynes his letter for Mr. Williams to read to the Sachem. So they returned back again, for I had said to them, that if they would go to Mantacut I would go likewise with them, and that Long-Island must not give wampum to Narraganset.

A while after this came Miantenomie from Block-Island to Mantacut with a troop of men, Waiandance being not at home; and instead of receiving presents, which they used to do in their progress, he gave them gifts, calling them, "brethren and friends; for so are we all Indians as the English are, and say brother to one another; so must we be one as they are, otherwise we shall be all gone shortly, for you know our fathers had plenty of deer and skins, our plains were full of deer, as also our woods, and of turkies, and our coves full of fish and fowl. But these English having gotten our land, they with scythes cut down the grass, and with axes felled the trees; their cows and horses eat the grass, and their hogs spoil our clam banks, and we shall all be starved; therefore it is best for you to do as we, for we are all the sachems from east to west, both Mouquakues and Mowhauks joining with us, and we are all resolved to fall upon them all, at one appointed day; and therefore I am come to you privately first, because you can persuade the Indians and Sachem to what you will, and I will send over fifty Indians to Block-Island, and thirty to you from thence, and take an hundred of South-ampton Indians with an hundred of your own here; and when you see the three fires that will be made forty days hence, in a clear night; then do as we, and the next day fall on and kill men women, and children, but no cows, for they will serve to eat till our deer be increased again." And our old men thought it was well.

So the Sachem came home and had but little talk with them, yet he was told there had been a secret consultation between the old men and Miantenomie, but they told him nothing in three days. So he came over to me and acquainted with the manner of the Narragansets being there with his men, and asked me what I thought of it; and I told him that the Narraganset Sachem was naught to talk with his men secretly in his absence, and bid him go home, and told him a way how he might know all, and then he should come and tell me; and so he did, and found all out as is above written, and I sent intelligence of it over to Mr. Haynes and Mr. Eaton; but because my boat was gone from home it was fifteen days before they had any letter, and Miantenomie was gotten home before they had the news of it. And the old men, when they saw how I and the Sachem had beguiled them, and that he was come over to me, they sent secretly a canoe over, in a moon-shine night, to Narraganset to tell them all was discovered; so the plot failed, blessed be God, and the plotter, next spring after, did as Ahab did at Ramoth-Gilead.—So he to Mohegin, and there had his fall.

Two years after this, Ninechrat sent over a captain of his, who acted in every point as the former; him the Sachem took and bound and brought him to me, and I wrote the same to Governor Eaton, and sent an Indian that was my servant and had lived four years with me; him, with nine more, I sent to carry him to New-Haven, and gave them food for ten days. But the wind hindered them at Plum-Island; then they went to Shelter-Island, where the old Sachem dwelt—Waiandance's elder brother, and in the night they let him go, only my letter they sent to New-Haven, and thus these two plots was discovered; but now my friend and brother is gone, who will now do the like?

But if the premises be not sufficient to prove Waiandance a true friend to the English, for some may say he did all this out of malice to the Pequits and Narragansets; now I shall prove the like with respect to the Long-Islanders, his own men. For I being at Meantacut, it happened that for an old grudge of a Pequit, who was put to

death at Southampton, being known to be a murderer, and for this
his friends bear spite against the English. So as it came to pass at
that day I was at Mantacut, a good honest woman was killed by
them at Southampton, but it was not known then who did this murder. And the brother of this Sachem was Shinacock Sachem could or
would not find it out. At that time Mr. Gosmore and Mr. Howell,
being magistrates, sent an Indian to fetch the Sachem thither; and
it being in the night, I was laid down when he came, and being a
great cry amongst them, upon which all the men gathered together,
and the story being told, all of them said the Sachem should not go,
for, said they, they will either bind you or kill you, and then us, both
men, women and children; therefore let your brother find it out, or
let them kill you and us, we will live and die together. So there
was a great silence for a while, and then the Sachem said, now you
have all done I will hear what my friend will say, for he knows what
they will do. So they wakened me as they thought, but I was not
asleep, and told me the story, but I made strange of the matter, and
said, "If the magistrates have sent for you why do you not go?"
They will bind me or kill me, saith he. "I think so," said I, "if
you have killed the woman, or known of it, and did not reveal it;
but you were here and did it not. But was any of your Mantauket
Indians there to-day?" They all answered, not a man these two
days, for we have inquired concerning that already. Then said I,
"did none of you ever hear any Indian say he would kill English?"
No, said they all; then I said, "I shall not go home 'till to-morrow,
though I thought to have been gone so soon as the moon was up, but
I will stay here till you all know it is well with your Sachem; if
they bind him, bind me, and if they kill him, kill me. But then you
must find out him that did the murder, and all that know of it, them
they will have and no more." Then they with a great cry thanked
me, and I wrote a small note with the Sachem, that they should not
stay him long in their houses, but let him eat and drink and be gone,
for he had his way before him. So they did, and that night he found
out four that were consenters to it, and knew of it, and brought them
to them at Southampton, and they were all hanged at Harford,
whereof one of these was a great man among them, commonly called
the Blue Sachem.

A further instance of his faithfulness is this; about the Pequit war time one William Hamman of the Bay, killed by a giant-like Indian towards the Dutch. I heard of it, and told Waiandance that he must kill him or bring him to me, but he said it was not his brother's mind, and he is the great Sachem of all Long-Island, likewise the Indian is a mighty great man, and no man durst meddle with him, and hath many friends. So this rested until he had killed another, one Thomas Farrington. After this the old Sachem died, and I spake to this Sachem again about it, and he answered, He is so cunning that when he hears that I come that way a hunting, that his friends tell him, and then he is gone.—But I will go at some time when nobody knows of it, and then I will kill him; and so he did— and this was the last act which he did for us, for in the time of a great mortality among them he died, but it was by poison; also two thirds of the Indians upon Long-Island died, else the Narragansets had not made such havoc here as they have, and might not help them.

And this I have written chiefly for our own good, that we might consider what danger we are all in, and also to declare to the country that we had found an heathen, yea an Indian, in this respect to parallel the Jewish Mordecai. But now I am at a stand, for all we English would be thought and called Christians; yet though I have seen this before spoken, having been these twenty-four years in the mouth of the premises, yet I know not where to find, or whose name to insert, to parallel Ahasuerus lying on his bed and could not sleep, and called for the Chronicles to be read; and when he heard Mordecai named, said, What hath been done for him? But who will say as he said, or do answerable to what he did? But our New-England twelve-penny Chronicle is stuffed with a catalogue of the names of some, as if they had deserved immortal fame; but the right New-England military worthies are left out for want of room, as Maj. Mason, Capt. Undrill Lieut. Sielly, &c., who undertook the desperate way and design to Mistick Fort, and killed three hundred, burnt the fort and took many prisoners, though they are not once named. But honest Abraham thought it no shame to name the confederates that helped him to war when he redeemed his brother Lot; but Uncas of Mistick, and Waiandance, at the Great Swamp and ever since your trusty friend, is forgotten, and for our sakes persecuted to this day with fire and sword, and Ahasuerus of New-England is still asleep, and if there be any like to Ahasuerus, let him remember what glory to God and honor to our nation hath followed their wisdom and valor.

Awake! awake Ahasuerus, if there be any need of thy seed or spirit here, and let not Haman destroy us as he hath done our Mordecai! And although there hath been much blood shed here in these parts among us, God and we know it came not by us. But if all must drink of this cup that is threatened, then shortly the king Sheshack shall drink last, and tremble and fall when our pain will be past.

O that I were in the countries again, that in their but twelve years truce, repaired cities and towns, made strong forts and prepared all things needful against a time of war like Solomon. I think the soil hath almost infected me, but what they or our enemies will do hereafter I know not. I hope I shall not live so long to hear or see it for I am old and out of date, else I might be in fear to see and hear that I think ere long will come upon us.

Thus for our tragical story, now to the comedy. When we were all at supper in the great hall, they the Pequits gave us alarm to draw us out three times before we could finish our short supper, for we had but little to eat, but you know that I would not go out; the reasons you know. 2ndly. You Robert Chapman, you know that when you and John Bagley were beating samp at the Garden Pales, the sentinels called you to run in, for there was a number of Pequits creeping to you to catch you; I hearing it went up to the redoubt and put two cross-bar shot into the two guns that lay above, and levelled them at the trees in the middle of the limbs and boughs, and gave order to John Frend and his man to stand with hand-spikes to turn them this or that way, as they should hear the Indians shout, for they should know my shout from theirs for it should be very short. Then I called six men and the dogs, and went out, running to the place, and keeping all abreast, in sight, close together. And when I saw my time, I said, stand! and called all to me saying, look on me; and when I hold up my hand, then shout as loud as you can, and when I hold down my hand, then leave; and so they did. Then

the Indians began a long shout, and then went off the two great guns
and tore the limbs of the trees about their ears, so that divers of
them were hurt, as may yet appear, for you told me when I was up
at Harford this present year, '60, in the month of September, that
there is one of them lyeth above Harford, that is fain to creep on all
four, and we shouted once or twice more; but they would not answer
us again, so we returned home laughing.

Another pretty prank we had with three great doors of ten feet
long and four feet broad, being bored full of holes and driven full
of long nails, as sharp as awl blades, sharpened by Thomas Hurlbut.—These we placed in certain places where they should come,
fearing least they should come in the night and fire our redoubt and
battery, or all the place, for we had seen their footing, where they
had been in the night, when they shot at our sentinels, but could not
hit them for the boards; and in a dry time and a dark night they
came as they did before, and found the way a little too sharp for
them; and as they skipped from one they trod upon another, and
left the nails and doors dyed with their blood, which you know we
saw the next morning laughing at it.

And this I write that young men may learn, if they should meet
with such trials as we met with there, and have not opportunity to
cut off their enemies; yet they may, with such pretty pranks, preserve themselves from danger,—for policy is needful in wars as well
as strength.

# CHAPTER III.

## *LETTERS TO JOHN WINTHROP, JR.*

The discovery of manuscripts in the handwriting of Lion Gardiner was a great surprise to his descendants and to students of our early colonial history. They appear to have been brought forth by unexpected hands from unexpected places. His "Relation of the Pequot Wars," first published in 1833, and his "Letters to John Winthrop, Jr.," first published in 1865, were found in the custody of strangers, yet rightfully possessed; having escaped fire and flood and avoided every other hazard for periods varying from one hundred and fifty-eight to two hundred and twenty-four years. The letters contained in this chapter are a part of the collection which have been published, from time to time, by the Massachusetts Historical Society under the designation of "Winthrop Papers" — being of a mass of manuscripts preserved for many generations by the Winthrop family of New London. Many of the letters of this collection bear dates from the earliest settlements in New England, and quite a number were written by eminent persons. The discovery of these manuscripts was made at the Winthrop residence on Fisher's Island in Long Island Sound in 1860; a large and valuable Island which was first purchased by John Winthrop, Jr., in 1644. It seems the existence of this collection was wholly unknown to the present generations; and the finding of them was unexpected; many of them were apparently in the same condition as when originally filed. As usual the historical society have printed these letters without corrections; and, consequently, the irregular orthography used by our ancestors in their carelessly written private letters, is made to appear as if on exhibition. The "Winthrop Papers" are invaluable to the student of New England affairs, and will be found in the Mass. Hist. Coll., Vols. VI and VII, 4th series, and I and VIII, 5th series.

[From the Collections of the Massachusetts Historical Society, Vol. VII. 4th Series, 52-65.]

### LION GARDINER TO JOHN WINTHROP, JR.

*To the Worshipfull Mr. John Winthrope Junior Esquire at Bostowne in the bay these present.*

WORSHIPFULL SIR,—I have received your letter, whearein I doe vnderstand that you are not like to returne, and according to your order I have sent your servaunts Robeart and Sara. I wonder that you did not write to me, but it is noe wonder, seeing that since your and Mr. Phenix departure, there hath beene noe provision sent, but, one the contrary, people to eate vp that small, now noe store, that wee had. Heare hath come many vessells with provision, to goe vp to the plantations, but none for vs. It seemes that wee have neather masters nor owners, but are left like soe many servaunts whose masters are willinge to be quitt of them; but now to late I wish that I had putt my thoughts in practice, that was to stay and take all such provisions out of the vessells, as was sufficent for a yeare; summer goods God's good providence hath not onely brought, but allso stayed, but if the could have gone, I did intent to have taken all the victualls out, and kept them for owre necesitie; and seeinge that you, Mr. Peeters, and Phenwicke knowes that it was agaynst my minde to send the Pequitts present agayne, and I with theas few men are, by your wills and likeings, put into a warlike condicion, there shall be noe cause to complayne of our ffidelitie and indeavours to you ward, and if I see that there be not such care for vs that owr lives may be preserved, then must I be fforced to shift as the Lord shall direct. I wish that it may be for God's glory and all your credits and proffitts. Heare is not 5 shillings of money and noe bevor. The Dutch man will bringe vs some corne and' rye, but we have noe thinge to pay him for it. Mr. Pinchin, had a bill to receive all the wampampeige we had; we have not soe much as will pay for the mendinge of our ould boate. I have sent your cowes vp to the plantations with 2 oxen; 2 of them we have killed and eaten, with the goates: a ramm goate was brought from the Manatos, but the enemie gott him and all the greate swine, 22, in one day, and had gotten all the sheep and cowes likewise, had we not sallid out. It was one of the Saboath day, and there was 4 men with the cowes with fierlocks. For the sheep, I have kept them thus longe, and when the pinckes comes downe I hope the will bringe hay for them for I haue not hay for them to eate by the way, if I should sent them to the bay; but now for our present condicion; since Mr. Phenwicke is gone for England, I hope you will not be fforgettfull of vs, and I thinke if you had not beene gone away and he had not come, we had not as yet beene at warrs with the Indians vppon such tearmes; they vp the river when I sent to them how it stood with vs, & in what need we weare, did jeare or mock vs, but time and patience will shew the efect of it. I heare that the Bachelor is to bringe vs provision, I pray you forgett vs not when shee comes from the Bermudas with some potates, for heare hath beene some Virginians that hath taught vs to plant them after a nother way, and I have put it in practise, and found it good. I pray you when you pay or recken with the owners of the pincke which brought the gunns heather, to shorten them for 3 weekes time and diet, for Sergant Tilley for pilat-einge the pincke vp with the cowes. I have, instead of your man Robert, hired Azarias for 20 shillings per moneth, or else I should not have let him come away. Heare is 2 men and ther wifes come from the Dutch plantation, a tayler and a shipp write, and I sett them boath to worke, but I have neather money nor victualls to pay them. I doe intend to sett the Dutch man to worke to make a Dutch smacke sayle, which shall carry 30 or 40 tun of goods, and not draw 3 foote and a halfe of water, principally to tranceport goods and passengers vp the river in safety. I pray lett us not want money or victualls, that some things may goe forward. Mr. Peeter say'd when he was heare that I should sell victualls to John Nott, Richard Graves, and them that came from the Dutch plantation, out of that little we had, and if all fayled he would supply vs with more, and fish like wise, to sell, but we have neather fish nor flesh to sell for others nor yet for [ourse] lves. Your wisdome will vnderstand the meaneinge of this writeinge.

At the closing of this letter came the cetch from the Naragansets with corne, and I haue tacken one hondard buchils of it, be caus I do not know whether we shall haue anie relief or not. Sum other small things of good-man Robbingson and John Charls I haue resauid, I pray yow fayl not to pay them. Thus with my loue to your selfe, your wife, ffather, mothar, and brethren, I reste yowrs

to cumand

LION GARDINER.

SAYBROOCK, this 6 of Novem, 1636. 1636.

We haue great cause of fear that William Quick with all the men & barke are taken by the Indians, coming downe the river; the Hope & they came downe togither from Watertowne, & came togither 20 mile. William Quick stayd there behind, & we fear went ashore a fowling. The Hope came in yesterday at noone, the wind hath been very faire to haue brought them downe euer since, & yet they are not come. We sadly fear the event: Pray for vs & consider, &c. &c. &c.

Nov: 7, late at night.

Immediately after the writing, this they came in dark night beyond expectation: but I thinke it would be good if no vessels may be suffred to come, but the men knowne & fitted with armes suitable, charg'd not to goe ashore, for they venture not onely their owne liues but wrong others also. The Indians are many hundreds of both sides the riuer, & shoote at our pinaces as they goe vp & downe, for they furnish the Indians with peeces, powder, & shot, & they come many times & shoot our owne pieces at vs, they haue 3 from vs, allready, 5 of Capt. Stones, one of Charles his, &c. Pardon our hast, &c. &c.

---

### LION GARDINER TO JOHN WINTHROP, JR.

*To the Worshipfull Mr. John Winthrop, at Boston, Ipsidge, or ese where, thes deliver.*

WORSHIPFULL SIR,—These are to certyfie you how the Lord hath beene pleased to deale with vs this winter: it hath pleased him, of his goodnes and mercy, to give vs rest from the Indians all this winter, butt one the 22th of the last moneth I, with tenn men more with me, went abou [e] our neck of land to fire some small bushes and marshes, whear we thought the enimie might have lien in ambush, and aboute halfe amile from home we started 3 Indians, and haveinge posibility to have cutt them short, we runinge to meett them, and to fire the marsh, but whylest our men was setteinge it one fire, there rushed out of the woods, 2 severall wayes, a great company of Indians, which though we gane fire vppon them, yett they run one to the very mussells of our peices, and soe the shott 3 men downe in the place, and 3 more men shott that escaped, of which one died the sam [e] night; and if the Lord had not putt it into my mind to make the men draw ther swords, the had taken vs all aliue, soe that sometime shouttinge and sometime retraightinge, keepinge them of with our sword [s,] we recovered a bayre place of ground, which this winter I had cleard for the same vse, and they durst not follow vs any further, because yt is vnder command of our great guns, of which I hope the have had some experience, as we heare by the relation of other Indians, and your friend Sacious and Nebott are the cheife actors of the treachery & villainy agaynst vs. As conceringe my sheep, which you writt to me of, I tooke order with Mr. Gibbins about them, but if he be not yett come home, I would intreat you that the may be kept with yours, untill you heare from him.   Thus hopeinge that you will be a meanes to stirr vp our friends in the bay, out of there dead sleep of securytie, to think that your condicon may be as ours is, vnles some speedy course be taken, which must not be done by a few, but by a great company, for all the Indiau[s] haue ther eyes fixed vppon vs, and this yeare the will all joyne with vs agaynst the Pequtt, and it is to be feared that the next year the will be agaynst vs.  We have vsed 2 sheets of your lead, which was in square $\frac{64}{104}$ foote.  I hav writ to the gouernour to pay you soe much agayne.  I haue sent you your bead steed, and would haue made a better, butt time would not permit, for we watch every other night, neuer puttinge of our clothes, for the Indians show themselves in troupes aboute vs, every day, as this bearer can certyfie you more at large.  Thus committinge you. your wife, father and mother, Mr. Peeter, and the rest of our friends, to God, I rest

Your asured frend to command

LION G[A]RDINER.<br>
1636.

SEABROOKE this 23th of the first moueth, 1636.

I mentioned that your lead was the one shiet 16 foot longe and 4 brood, the other 10 longe 4 brodd.

| 16 |   | 10 |
|----|---|----|
| 4  |   | 4  |
| 64 |   | 40 |
| 40 |   |    |

104 square foot.

Indorsed by J. Winthrop, jun., "Leift Leon Gardiner : "

---

LION GARDINER TO JOHN WINTHROP, JR.

*To his much honored ffrend Mr. John Winthrop at Nameag, dd.*

HONORED SIR,—I haue receiued yours by the Duchman, with the newes, for the which I humbly thanke you.  I sent you a bushell of hay seeds by Dauid Provost, a Duchman ; if you thinke that it will proue and sute your ground, you may haue more, if you please.

I heare you haue gotten sheepe: if you haue not a compleat English rame for them, I can lett you hane one which will bee a great advantage to you. This bearers, being our frends, desired me to write to you that thay might leaue their canow with you in safty, whilst thay goe to Mohegan, which I desier, and you shall command me as much in the like respect. I pray remember me to your wife and sister. Soe I rest

                                        LION GARDINER.

WIGHT, this 14th Aprill, 1649.

Indorsed by John Winthrop, jun., "Leift: Gardiner, Recd. Apr: 16:"

---

LION GARDINER TO JOHN WINTHROP, JR.

*To the worthyly Honnorid met. John Wthorp at his hows at Peqwit, theas present.*

1650, FROM THE ILE OF WIGHT, Aprill 27.

HONNORID SER,—I resavid yours by the Indian, with the hay seed, for which I kindly thanke yow; and for the cows that I have to sell, yow may have them. Thay ar ten, 5 on thier second or 3d califf, 5 heffers redi to calve. If yow will have all, when their calves ar wenid, yow may, or 5 now, the rest ten weeks hence, for fiftie pound, in good marchantabl wampem, bever, or silver; but if yow wil have them now, before the hefers have calvid, then I wil keep the 5 first calves, and their price is 55*li*. If my ocations wear not great, I wowld not sel som of them for 8*li*. a peece. As consurning the yong man yow writ of, this is our determination: not to have aboue 12 fasmilies, and wee know that we may pay as much as 24 in othar plasis, by reson of the fruitfulnes of our ground, and by reson that we ar to be but few, we ar resolvid not to resave anie. but such as ar fit for Cherch estate, being rethar wiling to part with sum of theas hear, then to resave more without good testimonie. Att present wee ar willing to giue this man you writ of 20*li*. a year, with such diat as I myself eat, til we see what the Lord will do with vs; and being he is but a yong man, hapily he hath not manie books, thearfore let him know what I have. First, the 3 Books of Martters,

Erasmus, moste of Perkins, Wilsons Dixtionare, a large Concordiance, Mayor on the New T[e]stement; some of theas, with othar that I have, may be veefull to him. I pray you, for the Lord sake, do what you can to get him hathar, and as I am ingagid to you allredie, so shall I be more

Yours to comand in the Lord,<br>
LION GARDENER.

I pray you send me word speedily about the cows, for els I must dispoes of them othar ways.

---

LION GARDINER TO JOHN WINTHROP, JR.

*To the worthyly honnored John Winthorp Esquire, at Peqwit, theis present.*

HONNORID SER,—My loue and sarvis bing remembrid to yow and al yours, ar theas to intreat yow to send me word whethar thear be anie hope of the man of Sitient, whome yow writt to me of; if not him, whethar yow hear of anie othar that might serue vs. I pray yow consider our conditon, and though wee might be forgit of yow loue and care for vs, yet the Lord wil not, whoes caws it is. Thus, in haste, I comit yow to the protextion of him that watchith over Israell, and rest

Yours by his help,<br>
LION GARDENER.

WIGHT, this 10th Agust, 1650.

Indorsed by John Winthrop, Jun., " Leift: Gardener."

---

LION GARDINER TO JOHN WINTHROP, JR.

FROM THE ILE OF WIGHT, this 22th of November, 1651."

HONNORED SIR,—My loue and sarvice being remembrid to you and yours, ar theas to let you know that I am myndid sudenly to sell 20 or 30 pounds worth of sheep, and having this opertunitie, I

6

thought to profer them to yow, knowing that thay ar of a better kinde then yours ar, espeshally if yow think fit to take a ram or 2 of mine, & sarve your other sheep with them, but that at your owne choys. Now if yow pleas to haue them, the pay that I desyar for them is marchantable wampem, or buttar at the ordenarie price, 6 pence a lb., the wampem to be payd to Martin Cruyer, the Duch man, when he cums in the s[p]ring to Goodman Stanton, or buter to him when he thinks fit to fetch it; but if you minde not to have them, then, let Goodman Stanton have the next profer, and let me have a flat yea or nay by this bearar, Goodman Bond. Thus in haste, I rest

Yours to be comandid,

LION GARDENER.

Indorsed by John Winthrop, jun., "Lt. Gardiner."

---

LION GARDINER TO JOHN WINTHROP, JR.

*To his worthily honored John Winter, Esq. at his house in Pequit, these present.*

FFROM THE ILEAWEIGHT, this 21 Ffebruary, 1651.

HONERED SIR,—My loue and seruice being remembred to you and yours, hoping of your health, as we are all at present, God be praysed; these are to let you know that all yours sheepe ewes which were marked for you, according to your order, by goodman Bond, on Saturday last were all well and in good case, and we looke for lambes the begginning of March, therefore you may order it as you see good, for the fetching of them away. I desire that you would satisfie Captaine Cryar with 30 pound of good wampom, for I haue depended upon it, and, if there be any oppertunity, I pray you to send me ten or twenty bushells of Indian meale, and I shall returne you, either barly, molt, or wampom. I should intreat you that these bags of wheat that I now send may be returned the first oppertunity, for we are in want of meale. Thus hoping to see you heere when you fetch the sheepe, I committing [*sic*] you to the Lord and rest

Yours by his helpe,

LION GARDENER.

Indorsed by John Winthrop, jun., "Leift. Gardiner, wherein his order for the payment of 30*li.* to Mr. Creiger."

LION GARDINER TO JOHN WINTHROP, JR.

*To the worthyly Honord John [Winthrop] Esqr.*

HONORED SIR,—I expected you heere the last weeke. The Mian-taquit Sachem told me, that you would come to fetch the sheepe, but hauing this oppertunity, I sent these 3 bags more, that if you haue any corne, I desire you to fill my bags, and send them by Joseph Garlicke, and if you haue none, speake to Thomas Stanton to fill them; and when you come for the sheepe we will make all strait on all sides. If there be any salt, I desire you to send me 2 or 3 bushells: thus hoping to se you heere, I rest

Yours to command,

LION GARDENER.

Indorsed by John Winthrop, Jun., "Mr. Lion Gardiner."

---

LION GARDINER TO JOHN WINTHROP, JR.

FROM THE ILE OF WIGHT, this last of Febrewari, 1652.

HONORID SIR,—My loue and sarvis being remembrid, ar theas to thank you for the hay seeds you sent me. I sowid them then, and sum came up. I have sent you a rariti of seeds which came from the Mouhaks, which is a kinde of milions, but far exelith all othar. They ar as good as weat frowar to thikin milk, and swet as sugar, and bakid thay [are] most exelent, having no shell. You may keep them as long as anie pumkins. And whereas you formarly spake to me to get you sum shels, I have sent you non by Goodman Garlick 1200, and allso 32 shilings in good wampem, desyaring you, if pos-ible, to send me 2 or 3 bushils of sumar wheat that is clean, without smut for seed; for I plowid not a foot of ground the last year, and now would fain sow sum that is clear of smut. I have one bagg with you still, and have sent 3 more, desiaring to fill them with meall and no peas, and if you wil be pleasid to balance our small acounts, what is dew to you, I will send, or if yow wil take anie goods of Martin Cruyar, charge it on my acount, and I wil pay him, and if anie opertewniti aford, hearafter, you may send me meall at all times, and I shall be redie to make pay to your desiar. Thus hoping to see you shortly, I comit yow to the Lord, and rest, evar

Yours,         LION GARDENER.

My wife desiarith Mistris Lake to get hur a dusen of trays, for shee hearith that thear is a good tray maker with you, and shee or will send him pay, or let Martin Cruyar, if he lyke anie thing he brings.

The shels cost me 30 shillings, the wampem in the bag, 32.

Indorsed by John Winthrop, jun., " L: Gardiner."

---

LION GARDINER TO JOHN WINTHROP, JR.

*To his worthyly honnorid frind, John Winthorp, Esqu. theas present, Pequoit.*

HONNORID SER,—My lone and sarvis being remembrid, ar theas to let you know that I resavid the 2 bushils of Indian meall by Cap. Sibada, in your sak, and have sent in it 3 bushils of malt, and 4 more in a sak of myne onne, and is all that I have at present. I thought to have sent yow sum barly to have maltid thear, becaws it is far better then the last year, but not knowing your minde, let it alone. I pray you send me what Indian meall yow can in the bags and emti barils, and what is in the bags and what in the barils a part. Conserning your sheep, thay ar all alyve, and though I have lost a great manie lambs this year, and never lost anie before, yet yours is a sofitient increas. Thus in haste, I rest yours to vce,

LION GARDENER.

APRILL 5, 1652.

If you have no store of Indian, I pray you speak to Thomas Stanton, to send me 8 bushiles.

Indorsed by John Winthrop, jun., "Leift. Gardiner."

LION GARDINER TO JOHN WINTHROP, JR.

*To the much honored Gouernor John Winthrope att Conellicutt, these dd.*

HONORED SIR,—I haue made bould to write vnto you a line ore to. So it is, that, by a neybour of yours it was propounded vnto me the sale of my Iland, but I hauing children and children's children, am not minded to sell it att present; butt I haue another plac, (I suppose) more convenient for the gentleman that would buy, liinge vpon Long Iland, betweene Huntington & Setokett: onely I thought good to make you acquainted with it, because I would not willingly be a means of bringing any into these parts, that would not like you and my ould freinds in this riuer; and therefore, if you & Mr. Willis & Mr. Allen, Mr. Stone, & other of my freinds like nott the buisnes, I can yett stop. If it be thought he wilbe as cordiall to you as I haue beene & yet am, it shal be, otherwise not. So desiring, when you can haue opertunty, to lett me vnderstand your mind herein. I rest

Yours in what duty and service I can,

LION GARDENER.

His name is Mr. Daniell Searle.

NOVEMB. 5. 1660.

Indorsed by John Winthrop, jun., "Lieft: Gardiner about sale of land vpon Long Iland betweene Huntington & Setuket, to the Governor of Barbados that then was, Mr. Serle."

---

[From the Collections of the Massachusetts Historical Society, I, 5th Series, 385-7.]

LION GARDINER TO JOHN WINTHROP, JR.

*To the worthyly honored John Winthrope, Esquire, Gouerner of the jurisdiction of Conneclicut, Hartforde, these prst.*

[MARCH, 1659-60?]

RIGHT WORTHY & HONERED FRIEND, MR WINTROP,—After my seruice presented, these few lines salute yow. These are to aquaint your worship that I receued your letter bearing date Desember the

12, wherin your worship desired to know the ocation of my stoping
a vesell, seiced by twoe of Capt Pennys sarnants of North Sea, coming to my Iland vpon ocation. I stopt her, vidz. the vesell, vpon
complant of my naghbour. John Scot informed mee they had taken
his vesell from of his own land, & that in the name of the Kinge of
Portinggale, vsing no other name when they seiced her. Vpon this
complant, I examened & found it acording to my naghbours information, for these tow men, vidz. Grigis & Hause, owned they had
neither commission nor coppie about them to act by, but sayd it
was in one of ther chests, vidz. Grigis, abord a ship with his name
in it, from the Portinggal imbasadore, which was ther master, &
that they toke her one ther owne acount, & had noe relation to anny
other, & that they would bring their commission within ten days or
forfit 2 hundred ponds & set free the vesell & goods, pay all just
damages to the ownere of the vesell & the owner of the goods, if
they brought not ther commision acording to ther time aboue mentioned. Then I gaue them 20 days time more then thay desiared, &
this they did frely, without any compulsion, & thay weare noe prisoners one my Ilande, but had giuen pasage with what help I could
aford them to Long Iland by a conoue, & thay were bound joyntly
& senerely, & one of the parties returnd again to the ship to Oyster-
bay, 12 days before ther bond was out, which is not aboue 70 miles
distant from Sowthampton or North Sea, to which place thaye ingaged to haue theyr Portinggale commission, & proue her pris by
ther commision, or set her free & neuer lay claim to her; but they
cam not acording to couenant by 7 days, & when they cam brought
noe commision with them, & then cam & demanded the vesell that I
had taken from them, as they were Capt Pennys sernants. My
answer was, I never heard the name of Capt Penny ore the state of
England. Soon after this ther com one George Lee, with a letter of
aturney from Capt Penny, & commenced an action against mee, laying to my carge damege to the valie of 500 ponds. The Court saw
cause not to meddle with the bisines, but bound mee oner to Hartforde to your worships for trial, & to apear the 17th of March, 1659·
Vpon the fourfetour of 2 hundred ponds to George Lee, I being de-
fectiue by my not apearinge acording to time, and hee was ingaged
in the sam sum set, he not apearing. The 17th of this instant, John

Scot being their, hee tendered his bond or staning security to answer
for George Lee, but that would not satisfye. I prefered to bee bound
for him my self, but nothinge would satesfy but I was the man they
amed at. Thus am I wronged by being exposed to a great danger,
in regard of my age & great weaknes, & inforsed to com ouer in such
a boat as by seamen, inhabitants of Saybrook, whoe serched the
vesell, promised they would not haue crosed the Sound in her, as I
had don, for all my estate. Thus is your pour sernant abused for
doeing an act of justes. Thus with my serues to you & your wif
remembered, I rest

Your asured louing freind to command to my power,

LION GARDENER.

# BIOGRAPHY.

---

The battles, sieges, fortunes, I have passed.—*Shakespeare*.

# BIOGRAPHY.

## CHAPTER I.

### THE FAMILY NAME.

To find out the true originall of surnames is full of difficultie.—CAMDEN.

The name Gardiner (1) may be derived from two Saxon words, *gar*, signifying a weapon, dart, javelin, arms; and *dyn*, signifying a sound, noise, alarm. Thus, Ed-*gar* signifies a happy weapon, literally the peaceable; Ethel-*gar* signifies a noble weapon, literally the magnanimous; *Gar*-far, a martial way, that is a military appearance; *Gar*-field, a martial place, that is a military encampment; *Gar-dyn*, a martial sound, that is a clashing of arms. The words *Gar* and *dyn*, with the English termination *er*, denoting the inhabitant of a place, make *Gar-dyn-er*. By an easy and natural transition of the *y* in *dyn* to *i*, it makes GARDINER.

Again, the name may be derived from the same roots as *Gairdin*, which, in the Gaelic language, signifies an inclosed place, a beacon hill; from *Gair*, an out-cry, and *din*, a hill, literally a fortification. Add to *Gairdin* the termination *er* and it makes *Gairdin-er*. The English pronunciation of *Gairdiner* would soon lead to dropping the *i* in the first syllable, which would make it GARDINER.

Again, the name may be derived from an occupation, the keeper of a garden, as *Garden-er*, which subsequently may have been

(1) The materials for this chapter have been mostly drawn from "An Etymological Dictionary of Family Names," by William Arthur, M. A. His eldest son Chester A. Arthur, President of the United States, contributed the introductory Essay, showing rare literary ability, and a marked degree of research and ingenuity, interspersed with humor, yet his name does not appear in the work, being at the time of its publication a young lawyer in the city of New York. It is pertinent to our subject to remark that the first law firm formed by young Arthur was Messrs. Arthur & Gardiner, which was continued until dissolved by the death of his partner, Mr. Henry D. Gardiner, who was a descendant of Lion Gardiner.—C. C. G.

changed from *Gardener* to GARDINER, that the occupation and the name of a person might be the more readily distinguished. (1)

Camden's Remaines, *printed at London, 1614,* relates that a book had been written against Stephen Gardiner, Bishop of Winchester, by a brother prelate, in which the supposed origin of Gardiner's name was sneeringly alluded to; "at which time," Camden says, "wise was the man who told my Lord Bishop that his name was not Gardener, as the English pronounce it, but Gard*i*ner, with the French accent, *and therefore a gentleman.*"

(1) The name Gardiner, Gardener and Gardner can be traced to a very early period in England. Emigrants of the name came to New England with the earliest Puritans. The Mayflower brought one, and others came a decade before Lion Gardiner. It cannot be ascertained that any of the early arrivals were related by the ties of consanguinity. The popular belief that the spelling of a family name indicates relationship is not well founded. Only authenticated records can be relied upon to make proof of pedigrees.—C. C. G.

## Fac Simile of Signature and Seal.

Attached to letter dated Saybrooke, November 6th, 1634.

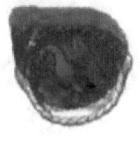

HERALDIC DESCRIPTION: Pelican Vulning Herself.

# LION GARDINER, 1599–1663.

*This seal was probably borrowed from Thomas Pell, who was a surgeon for the garrison at Saybrook Fort. The Pellforest is a pelican. (Sarah D. Gardiner.)*

## THE PELICAN IN HERALDRY.

C. C. G.

HERALDRY.—The Pelican when represented in profile she is "vulning herself," and when in full face on her nest feeding her young, she is "in her piety."—*Encyclopedia Britannica*, Vol. XI, p. 701.

The Pelican is always represented with her wings endorsed, neck embowed, and picking her breast, from which issue drops of blood.—*Encyclopedia of Heraldry*, by John Burke, p. XXII.

The young Pelican is fed by the regurgitated food of its mother; hence arose the poetic idea of the ancients, that she nourished her young with her blood.—*The American Cyclopedia*, Vol. VIII, p. 296.

# CHAPTER II.

## THE FAMILY ARMS.

Every man of the children of Israel shall pitch by his own standard,
with the ensign of their father's house.—NUMBERS II, 2.

The use of particular symbols by nations, families and individuals is very ancient. Heraldry is purely a feudal institution, and had its origin in the necessity of adopting some device to distinguish persons concealed in armor in battles and at tournaments, which was gradually elaborated during the Crusades. The Normans introduced it into England. As a system, bound by certain rules and forms, with technical nomenclature, it can be traced to the thirteenth century, when arms began to be displayed on coins, monumental brasses and tombs, and in architectural decorations, and on shields and surcoats. From their use on garments is derived the phrase "coat of arms."

### FRONTISPIECE.

ARMS—Argent a chevron between three buglehorns stringed gules.
CREST—An arm in armor hand grasping the broken shaft of a lance.

Our frontispiece represents a coat of arms which indicates great antiquity to the family bearing them. The form of the shield and the drapery surrounding it have no heraldic significance. The Helmet shows the rank, and the emblems depicted on the Shield together with the figure representing the Crest, constitute the armorial insignia. The *Chevron* is one of the honorable "ordinaries" in heraldry, adopted from the bow of the ancient war saddle, which rose high in front. The *Buglehorn* is one of the important "charges" in heraldry.

The word bugle is derived from the Latin *buculus*, signifying an ox. The first bugles were probably formed from ox horns, and were brought into use by shepherds to call their flocks, by hunters to wind in the chase, and by warriors to signal for battle. The *Crest* was introduced subsequent to the first bearing of arms, and the ornament selected for it usually had reference to the act for which the honor was conferred. The arm is frequently employed as a figure of strength. A Crest represented by "an arm in armor hand grasping the broken shaft of a lance," indicates that it was worn by a warrior of great power, who was skilled in the use of the lance, and famed for disarming his opponent.

### THE FATHERS' AVERSION TO TITLES AND ARMS.

The Fathers of New England established a government on the basis of equality, and consequently were averse to recognizing distinctions of rank and hereditary titles and the appendages to them, including coats of arms which were looked upon as the finery of princes and bauble of the gentry; as impracticable, yet harmless things. Their aversion to rank and titles was transmitted to succeeding generations, and ultimately found expression in the text of our national constitution, which declares that no title of nobility shall be granted, and no person holding an office shall accept of a title from any foreign state. Their repugnance to coats of arms does not appear to have been of a very pronounced character, probably because there were but few in the country, and none were ostentatiously displayed.

Disuse, neglect and lapse of time have made it difficult to trace some of those which have been preserved to an undoubted ancestor who rightfully bore them.

### LION GARDINER'S FAMILY ARMS.

It is believed that Lion Gardiner was descended from a family that had a coat of arms. The ground for this belief rests upon undoubted proof that he was a gentleman, as the term was applied to those having coats of arms and of the middle rank in England; and, furthermore, upon the fact that his descendants have been in possession of a coat of arms for many generations, bearing the tradition that they were our Gardiner Arms.

There is no evidence showing that arms were ever borne by Lion Gardiner, nor by his son David Gardiner. Only a bible is claimed to have been handed down from Lion, and absolutely nothing is known to have come down from David.

### EARLIEST KNOWN DISPLAYS OF OUR GARDINER ARMS.

The earliest known display of our Gardiner Arms were those placed on the tombstone of John Gardiner, the eldest grandson of Lion, and third proprietor. (1) That tombstone was erected in the old burying ground at New London, Ct., where it remains in a fair state of preservation. It consists of a plain brown stone slab, placed horizontally over the grave, and supported on stone pillars. Near the head of the slab there is a square piece of *new* slate-stone, imbedded and cemented in the top, on which is graven a strange coat of arms. Then follows the inscription. (2)

(1) The arms displayed on this tomb, at that time, were unquestionably our Gardiner Arms, for no other arms were known in the family until a later period. This John Gardiner's Will provides that he "shall be decently buried, at the discretion of his executors," who were Nathaniel Huntling, Jr., and William Hedges, Jr., both of East Hampton, L. I. As he died suddenly at New London, the probability is that the place of his interment and the tomb, inscription and arms were agreed upon by the executors and the testator's family.— C. C. G.

(2) ARMS ON OLD SLATE-STONE, WITH INSCRIPTION.　　ARMS ON NEW SLATE-STONE, WITH INSCRIPTION

HERE LYETH BURIED YE BODY OF HIS EXCELLENCY JOHN GARDINER, THIRD LORD OF YE ISLE OF WIGHT. HE WAS BORN APRIL 19TH, 1661, AND DEPARTED THIS LIFE JUNE 25TH, 1738.

HERE LYETH BURIED YE BODY OF HIS EXCELLENCY JOHN GARDINER, THIRD LORD OF YE ISLE OF WIGHT. HE WAS BORN APRIL 19TH, 1661, AND DEPARTED THIS LIFE JUNE 25TH, 1738.

8

At New London there is a well authenticated tradition concerning this tombstone, which runs this wise: " When first erected there was a piece of slate imbedded in the slab, occupying the same space which is now filled by the *new* slate, on which was graven the Gardiner Arms. Some time prior to the present century the *old* piece of slate was ruthlessly taken out and carried away, and the vacant space was not occupied till filled by the *new* slate very recently." It is not known who removed the *old* slate, but, unquestionably, kinsmen (?) directed the putting in of the *new* slate.

At New London, Mrs. Coit, *nee* Brainard, wife of Hon. Robert Coit, (1) has in her possession the original Will of John Gardiner, third proprietor. Also a very old representation of our Gardiner Arms, painted in water colors on parchment; showing a shield emblazoned with the arms which with helmet, crest and mantlings are done with the proper metals and colors; and the heraldic description written underneath the shield, thus: "He beareth argent a chevron gules between three buglehorns stringed sable." The whole fabric being inclosed, under glass, in a gilded frame 14 by 18 inches, which hangs squarely against the wall. Mrs. Coit has a number of very old looking prints of the same arms taken on paper from copperplate, which have the name *John Gardiner* engraved, in script, underneath the shield.

The Will, and the painted arms, and the printed arms were all received by Mrs. Coit from her great aunt, Mary Gardiner, b. 1769, d. 1858, who never married, and who was a daughter of John Gardiner, the only son of Jonathan Gardiner, one of the sons of John Gardiner, third proprietor.

The tradition concerning the painted arms is that they have

(1) Mr. Robt. Coit graduated at Yale College, and is a lawyer, and has been Mayor of New London, Judge of Probate, Member of the House and of the Senate in the Legislature of Connecticut, and is one of the best known and influential citizens of New London, now in his fifty-fourth year. His great grandmother, on his father's side, was Mary Gardiner, b. 1744, d. 1824, a daughter of David Gardiner, who was a son of David Gardiner, fourth proprietor. She married Thomas Coit, M. D., b. 1725, d. 1811. Mrs. Robt. Coit's great grandmother, on her father's side, was Sarah Gardiner, a daughter of John Gardiner, who was the only son of Jonathan Gardiner, a son of John Gardiner, third proprietor. She married Judge Jeremiah Gates Brainard, b. 1760, d. 1830, a distinguished citizen of New London. Mrs. Coit's father was a brother of Connecticut's highly gifted poet, John Gardiner Coit Brainard, b. 1796, d. 1828, who departed this life far too soon for his own fame.

been handed down many generations; from a period so remote that the name of the ancestor who bore them is not remembered. It has been the custom to speak of these painted arms as the original arms, implying thereby that they were the first of our arms known in this country, and from which copies had been taken.

At the Gardiner's Island residence, Mr. J. Lyon Gardiner, twelfth proprietor, (1) has in his possession our Gardiner Arms embroidered on black satin, showing a shield emblazoned with the arms, which, with the helmet, crest and mantlings, are worked in the proper metals and colors. The material representing the face of the shield is silvered thread, while that representing the chevron and buglehorns is black sewing silk; the helmet is made of golden thread on a light blue silk field, and the crest is of light blue and white silk, except the staff, which is of silvered thread. The whole fabric being inclosed under glass in a mahogany and gilt lozenge-shaped frame, 23 by 23 inches square, which hangs against the wall, over the parlor mantel. The island tradition (2) is that this piece of needlework was executed by a daughter of David Gardiner, fourth proprietor, while she was attending school in Boston. The fourth proprietor had three daughters, and the advanced school age of either of them occurred after 1730. Also, a number of small prints, of the same arms, taken on paper from copper-plate, which were engraved and printed under the direction of John Lyon Gardiner, seventh proprietor, and by him pasted on the front covers of the books in his library. These prints are a near fac simile of the prints in the possession of Mrs. Coit, at

(1) Mr. J. Lyon Gardiner, twelfth proprietor, purchased the island of his brother, Mr. David J., late eleventh proprietor, who acquired it by the will of his father, the late Samuel B., tenth proprietor. A Notice of Gardiner's Island will be found in the succeeding chapter.—C. C. G.

(2) On a visit to Gardiner's Island, August 9th and 10th, 1855, I met Mrs. Gardiner, widow of John Lyon, seventh proprietor, then in her seventy-fourth year, and her sons Mr. John G., ninth proprietor, and Mr. Samuel B., and his daughter, of East Hampton, L. I. On the subject of the embroidered arms, which then hung in a frame over the parlor mantel, Mrs. Gardiner related the tradition; that the work was executed by a daughter of the fourth proprietor while attending school in Boston; her education cost more than the value of the cattle on the island; she was accomplished and attractive, but she disregarded the wishes of her parents by marrying the son of a poor minister. It is known that the fourth proprietor had a daughter named Mary who married Samuel, the son of Rev. Nathaniel Huntting of East Hampton, L. I.; and, it may be, that she was the accomplished maiden who embroidered the honored heir-loom, and married a husband of her own choice.—C. C. G.

New London. Also, within the family burying ground, the same
arms, graven on the tombstones of the fifth, sixth and seventh
proprietors. (1)

At Middletown, Ct., Rev. Thos. W. Coit, D. D., (2) has in his pos-

(1) Within the family burying ground at Gardiner's Island there are four tombstones which have
inscriptions with arms graven on them, namely:

### FOURTH PROPRIETOR.

INSCRIPTION AND ARMS ON A BROWN STONE
SLAB.

HERE LIES INTERRED THE REMAINS OF DAVID
GARDINER, ESQ., OF THE ILE OF WIGHT, WHO
DEPARTED THIS LIFE JULY 4, 1751, IN THE 61ST
YEAR OF HIS AGE.

#### NOTE.

The heraldic reading of the above arms are very
like the arms of Richard Gardiner, D. D., third
Canon of Christ Church, Oxford, who died December 20, 1670, aged 79, which read thus: Sable a
chevron between two griffins heads erased in chief
and a cross patee in base or. Vide Wood's Athenæ
Oxonienses, Vol. III, p. 609.

The distinguished Canon who bore these arms
was born in Hereford, Herefordshire, and his
remains are buried in Christ Church Cathedral,
Oxford, where there is a Latin epitaph reciting
his many virtues. Was he a relative of Lion
Gardiner? There is no proof.—C. C. G.

### FIFTH PROPRIETOR.

INSCRIPTION AND CREST ON A BROWN STONE SLAB.

IN MEMORY OF JOHN GARDINER, ESQ., OF THE ILE
OF WIGHT, WHO DEPARTED THIS LIFE MAY THE
19TH. A. D. 1764, IN THE 50TH YEAR OF HIS AGE.

### SIXTH PROPRIETOR.

INSCRIPTION AND CREST ON A BROWN STONE SLAB.

HERE LIES THE BODY OF DAVID GARDINER, ESQ.,
OF THE ILE OF WIGHT, WHO DEPARTED THIS
LIFE SEPTEMBER 5TH, 1774, IN THE 36TH YEAR OF
HIS AGE.

### SEVENTH PROPRIETOR.

INSCRIPTION AND CREST ON A WHITE MARBLE
MONUMENT.

READER,
BENEATH THIS MARBLE ARE DEPOSITED THE
REMAINS OF JOHN L. GARDINER, ESQ., THE
SEVENTH PROPRIETOR OF GARDINER'S ISLAND,
BORN, NOVEMBER 8TH, 1770. DIED, NOVEMBER
22ND, 1816.

(2) Thomas Winthrop Coit, an American clergyman of the Episcopal Church. Born in New London,
Ct., June 28, 1803. Graduated at Yale College in 1821. Entered the ministry in 1827. Was President of Transyl-
vania University, Lexington, Ky., in 1854. Since 1854 has been professor in Berkley Divinity School,
Middletown, Ct. Dr. Coit ranks among the foremost of living scholars in the Episcopal Church, and is the
author of several works in defense of its doctrines and position.—[The American Cyclopedia, Vol. V. p. 53.

session our Gardiner Arms quartered with the Coit Arms, embroidered on black satin; the Gardiner Arms occupying the dexter chief and sinister base; the shield, showing the quartered arms, crest, mantlings and motto, worked in the proper metals and colors; the whole fabric being inclosed in a lozenge-shaped frame, 22 by 22 inches square, which hangs against the wall. The *Crest* belongs to the Gardiner Arms, and the *Motto*, Virtus sola nobilitas, to the Coit Arms. Dr. Coit states that these arms were the handwork of his grandmother, Mary Gardiner, b. 1744, d. 1824, the wife of Thos. Coit, M. D., b. 1725, d. 1811, and a daughter of David Gardiner, one of the sons of David Gardiner, fourth proprietor. The work was executed when his grandmother was quite young, and he has a clear recollection of seeing the arms when a child, during the lifetime of his grandmother, while in the possession of his uncle, Jonathan Coit, and still later in the possession of his unmarried sister, Mary G. Coit, from whose effects he procured them by purchase.

## THE EDITOR'S CONCLUSIONS.

Our first inquiry will be directed to the evidence introduced into this chapter bearing respectively upon the two different representations of arms shown.

*First*, The Arms which read, " Sable a chevron between two griffins heads erased in chief and a cross formée in base or," are displayed on the tombstone of David Gardiner, fourth proprietor, at Gardiner's Island; and *now* on the tombstone of John Gardiner, third proprietor, at New London. These arms bear no tradition and have no record, and no one has ever been able to explain why they were placed on the tomb of a descendant of Lion Gardiner.

*Second*, The Arms which read, "Argent a chevron between three buglehorns stringed gules. *Crest*, an arm in armor hand grasping the broken shaft of a lance," are those which were at *first* displayed on the tombstone of John Gardiner, third proprietor, at New London; and on the painted and printed representations in the possession of

Mr. and Mrs. Coit at New London; and on the embroidered and printed representations in the possession of Mr. J. Lyon Gardiner, twelfth proprietor, at Gardiner's Island; and on the tombstones of the fifth, sixth and seventh proprietors, at Gardiner's Island; and on the embroidered representation in the possession of Dr. Coit, at Middletown. These arms bear with them many concurring traditions of the most authentic character.(1)

In our opinion the most ancient of the several representations of arms, referred to in this chapter, are the painted and the printed displays in the possession of Mr. and Mrs. Coit at New London, which, we think, were once the property of John Gardiner, third proprietor. This belief is founded partly on conjectures and partly on the fact that the displays, themselves, appear to be of great age; but chiefly because the Will of the said John Gardiner and the Arms mentioned have been handed down together, as companion pieces, so to speak.

The next oldest display are the embroidered arms at Gardiner's Island; and the next, the embroidered arms at Middletown; and the last, the prints taken from copper-plate, which were executed under the direction of John Lyon Gardiner, seventh proprietor, as our Gardiner Arms. Our frontispiece is a fac simile of one of those prints. (2)

The Encyclopedia of Heraldry, Or General Armory of England, Scotland and Ireland, by John Burke, contains a registry of armorial bearings from the earliest time. In this work the name *Gardiner* has twenty-three separate and distinct registrations; the name *Gardener* has eight; the name *Gardner* has

(1) The representations of arms, particularly referred to in this chapter as our Gardiner Arms, are all exactly alike in what may be termed essentials; that is to say, they show the same emblems on the shield and the same ornament for the crest. In the tinctures, a term applied to metals, colors and furs in heraldry, there are slight variations—only however in the colors of the chevron and bugle-horns. These differences are hardly worth noticing; yet may be stated. The New London painted and printed arms show the chevron gules and the bugle-horns sable; the Gardiner's Island printed arms, from which our frontispiece was taken, show both the chevron and bugle-horns gules; while the Gardiner's Island embroidered arms, somewhat changed by age, show both the chevron and bugle-horns sable; the Middletown embroidered arms, considerably faded, show both the chevron and bugle-horns sable.—C. C. G.

(2) On my visit to Gardiner's Island, Mr. Samuel B. Gardiner presented to me one of the small prints of arms that were executed by the direction of his father, which I still possess. The fact that John Lyon, seventh proprietor, ordered a copper-plate engraving representing our Gardiner Arms, shows very pointedly that he took no notice of the graven symbols on the tomb of the fourth proprietor.—C. C. G.

twenty-two; the name *Gardenar* has one; the name *Gardinor* has one. Total, fifty-five. The description of our Gardiner Arms is not like either of the above fifty-five registrations. Several of them have the chevron between three buglehorns stringed, some with and some without crests, but our distinctive crest does not appear. Though our Gardiner Arms were identical with a registry at the College of Arms, it would still be difficult to claim them, by right of inheritance, without first establishing a pedigree from an undoubted ancestor, who bore them.

In our country, when it is ascertained that a coat of arms cannot be found in the registers of heralds, the defect is not considered as necessarily fatal to their legitimacy, provided there is proof to show they have been perpetuated, by the family claiming them, from a remote period.

Our old families usually hold these ancient ensigns as heir-looms, like old furniture, paintings, plate, books and other relics of the household, rather than as badges boastful of ancestral pride.

### LION GARDINER'S SIGNATURE AND A SEAL.

Personal seals were used before and after the introduction of armorial bearings in England.(1) Very probably Lion Gardiner had a private seal which he used for stamping letters and instruments in writing, as was customary with gentlemen. He may have used the crest of his family arms for a seal? There is a fac simile of his signature and of a seal attached to a certain letter of his, dated at Saybrooke, November 6th, 1636, addressed to John Winthrop, Jr., which can be found in the Appendix of Vol. VII, Fourth Series Massachusetts Historical Society Collections; and upon a leaf fronting the first page of this chapter. Unfortunately there is no proof showing that this particular seal was the property of Lion Gardiner. The mere fact that an impression of it was found

(1) The old common law definition of a seal is that given by Lord Coke: Sigillum est cera impressa.—"A seal is an impression in wax."—C. C. G.

stamped in wax on one of his letters does not establish any ownership.    Within the Appendix of the volume mentioned, as containing the fac simile of his signature and seal, there are fourteen
other signatures, of his contemporaries, which show two different
seals to each name; also three other signatures which show three
different seals to each name; and two other signatures which show
the same seal to each name; and many signatures without seals.
Therefore the presumption that either of the writers, of signatures
referred to, stamped their letters with their own seals, cannot be
sustained without extraneous proof.

# CHAPTER III.

## *BIOGRAPHICAL SKETCH OF LION GARDINER.*

We would speak first of the Puritans, the most remarkable body of men, perhaps, which the world has ever produced. * * * Those who aroused the people to resistance—who directed their measures through a long series of eventful years—who formed, out of the most unpromising materials, the finest army that Europe had ever seen—who trampled down king, church and aristocracy—who in the short intervals of domestic sedition and rebellion, made the name of England terrible to every nation on the face of the earth, were no fanatics. * * * If they were unacquainted with the works of philosophers and poets, they were deeply read in the oracles of God. If their names were not found in the registers of heralds, they felt assured that they were recorded in the Book of Life. If their steps were not accompanied by a splendid train of menials, legions of ministering angels had charge over them: their diadems crowns of glory which should never fade away.—LORD MACAULAY.

### I.—FOUNDERS OF NEW ENGLAND.

The Founders of New England belonged to that party of sturdy Englishmen which, early in the seventeenth century, distinguished itself by great pertinacity and courage in its repeated efforts in behalf of constitutional government and religious freedom. They were called Puritans. The first Puritan emigrants to New England embarked from Holland. They were the Pilgrim Fathers of the Plymouth Colony. The second company of Puritan emigrants, called "the great emigration," sailed from England, led by John Winthrop, the elder, and his associates of the Massachusetts Company. Closely following the Winthrop fleet, came Roger Williams, John Davenport, Henry Vane, Hugh Peters, John Winthrop, the younger, on his second voyage, and many others equally distinguished.

The earliest English soldier emigrant was Miles Standish, the valiant Captain of Plymouth. Later on came John Endicott, Israel Stoughton, John Mason, John Underhill, Edward Gibbons, Simon Willard, Robert Seeley and Lion Gardiner, all of whom participated in the early Indian wars in Connecticut.

These, with others, penetrated the wilderness, repelled the savages, formed the settlements, gathered the churches, kept the schools, made their own laws and governed themselves. They were the founders of New England.

The subject of this sketch was highly favored. He lived in one of the grand epochs of modern times—that which witnessed the rise of the Republic in Holland, the establishment of the Commonwealth in England and the colonization of the Puritans in New England, all links of one chain. (1)

## II.—LION GARDINER.

Lion Gardiner was a native of England. (2)  He was a gentleman, without title, of the middle rank between the nobility and yeomanry. His nativity is well authenticated, but his ancestry is not known, never having been successfully traced. (3)

He was born in the days of Good Queen Bess, and he attained his majority during the reign of the first English Sovereign of the unfortunate House of Stuart, in the same year which witnessed the embarkation of the Pilgrim Fathers for New England. At that time the implacable differences between the Established Anglican Church and the Protestant Dissenters deeply agitated England. Comprehending the gravity of affairs he was not content to be a mere spectator. In the struggle between the King and Parliament he adhered to the Parliament party, and was a Dissenter and a friend of the Puritans. It is probable that he was a younger son and went abroad early in life. Young and ambitious, his heart was set upon deeds of adventure; and, following the footsteps of many of his countrymen, he volunteered to maintain the republican standard in Holland.

England had been the ally of Holland in its greatest dangers.

(1) Motley's Rise of the Dutch Republic, Vol. 1, p. iv.

(2) One annotator calls Lion Gardiner a native of Scotland. Vide Mass. Hist. Coll. VII, 4th series, 52, note. The statement is not sustained by proof. In 1686 David, son of Lion Gardiner, in a petition to Gov. Dongan of New York, mentions his father as the first Englishman that had settled in that Province. Family tradition claims him as a native of England. Should there remain any doubt as to his nativity, his manuscript writings will settle the question. If his mother tongue was Scotch, it is nowhere shown in his words and phrases. Undoubtedly, therefore, he was of English descent.—C. C. G.

(3) One writer states that East Hampton, L. I., was first called Maidstone because Lion Gardiner and others came from Maidstone, County of Kent, England. (a)  Another writer states that some of the first settlers of East Hampton came from Sianstoft, County of Kent, and possibly some may have come from Maid-stone. (b)  The late James Savage of Boston, while on a visit to England in 1842, stated in his "Gleanings" : "Sir Thos. C. Banks, author of Dormant and Extinct Baronetcies of England wrote me: 'I suspect the family of Gardiner of Gardiner's Island to be the representatives of Mr. Gardiner who married one of the co-heiresses of the Barony, the most ancient Barony of Fitz Walter, now under claim before the House of Lords by Sir H. Brooke Bridges, Bart.' Fitz Walter was General of the Barons' army which obtained the Magna Charta of King John."—Mass. Hist. Coll., VIII, 3rd series, 310. All of the foregoing, it will be observed, are mere conjectures. Distinguished antiquarians and kinsmen, visiting England, have frequently searched among the repositories of counties and parishes, and consulted registers of heralds without any success whatever.—C. C. G.

(a) Thompson's His. L. I., 1, 296.

(b) J. L. Gardiner, Notes on East Hampton. Vide Doc. His. N. Y., I, 679.

Robert, Earl of Leicester. commanded the English forces there under Queen Elizabeth. English regiments had for a long period garrisoned some of its towns. Sir Thomas Fairfax, of the Scottish peerage, served there under the command of Lord Vere, in the reign of Charles the First; and, about that time. young Gardiner appeared with the same forces, a Lieutenant.

### III.—MILITARY SERVICE IN HOLLAND.

The years rolled on! A change and new honors awaited the young Lieutenant. "In 1635," Gardiner's own account states, (1) he was "an engineer and master of works of fortification in the legers of the Prince of Orange in the Low Countries." While there, certain eminent Puritans acting for a company of Lords and Gentlemen in England, approached him with an offer to go to New England and construct works of fortification and command them. The offer was accepted. through the "persuasions" of Hugh Peters. pastor of a church of English exiles at Rotterdam, and John Davenport, a dissenting minister from London, and "some other well-affected Englishmen of Rotterdam."

He contracted with the company "for £100 per annum for four years," and himself and family were to be furnished transportation and subsistence to the place of his destination; and he was to serve the company "only" in the "drawing, ordering and making of a city, towns or forts of defence," under the immediate direction of John Winthrop, the younger.

About the time he entered into this engagement, he was married to Miss Mary Wilemson of Woerdon, Holland.

### IV.—EMBARKS FOR NEW ENGLAND.

"On the tenth day of July, 1635," Gardiner and his wife left Woerdon, Holland, bound for New England via London. They took passage in the bark *Bachelor*, probably, at Rotterdam

(1) Vide His Relation of the Pequot Wars. Supra, p. 14 et seq. The same paper should be consulted for all quotations in this Chapter, not credited.—C. C. G.

In the Custom House at London, under date of August 11th, 1635, there is recorded the arrival of the *Bachelor*, with Gardiner and his wife and their maid and one other person, as passengers, "who are to pass to New England." (1)

Under date of London, August 16th, 1635, Edward Hopkins, agent for forwarding certain ships with supplies to the "Connecticut plantation" in New England, addressed a letter to John Winthrop, the younger, then on his way to New England, informing him that he had just cleared the "North Sea Boatt"—meaning the *Bachelor*—for New England. The passengers mentioned are Gardiner and his wife and their maid and his workmaster; the cargo is stated by item, and the master, together with the crew, are individually named. The passengers and crew numbered twelve persons. A postscript states that the *Bachelor* got off to sea at Gravesend August 18th, 1635. (2)

### V.—ARRIVAL AT BOSTON.

Governor Winthrop of Massachusetts, who kept a journal of the transactions in the colony, under the date of November 28th, 1635, mentions the arrival of a small bark sent over by Lord Say and others, with "Gardiner an expert engineer" and provisions of all sorts to begin a fort at the mouth of Connecticut River. (3)

Gardiner remained for some little time in Boston. The winter

(1) Extract from MS. volume in folio at the Augmentation Office where Rev. Joseph Hunter one of the Record Commissioners presides in Rolls Court, Westminster Hall, which contains the names of persons to embark at the Port of London after Christmas 1634 to the same period in the following year: "f°. 95. 11 Augti. in the Batcheler de Lo. Master, Tho: Webb vs New England. Lyon Gardner 36 yers & his wife Mary 34 yers & Eliza Coles 23 yers their maid servant & Wm Jope 40 yers who are to pass to New England have brought &c. &c. &c." Mass. Hist. Coll. VIII. 3rd series, 271. The conclusion of the foregoing record, if written out in full, would probably read, after the words "have brought," certificates from justice of the peace and minister of the parish of * * * of conformity; the men have taken the oath of supremacy and allegiance, and are not subsidies. As Gardiner had been abroad some years, and his wife a foreigner, it is probable they brought with them certificates, from a Calvinistic church in Holland, which was the national religion of that country, protected by the English Government, then at the head of the Protestant interest in Europe. The English Government persecuted Presbyterians at home, but extended a powerful protection to their churches abroad at that time.—C. C. G

(2) Extract of a letter from Edward Hopkins to John Winthrop, Jr., dated: "London the 16th of August 1635. Per the shipp Batcheler, whom God preserve: Mr. John Winthrop, Sir: * * * I have now cleared of from hence the North Sea Boatt" * * * It was nott easy here to get any att this tyme to goe in soe small a vessell * * * The master is able enough but savours nott godlinesse * * * Serieant Gardiner and Wm Job his workmaster with the Serieant's wiefe and his mayd came over in this barque"—i. e. over from Holland to London—C. 47. G (?) * * * "They are all to be at the Companies charge for matter of diett. The Serieant hath receaved of me beforehand towards his first year's wages 8£. sterlinge, & Wm Job hath receaved 15£., the master also of the barque hath receaved 8£." * * * Mass. Hist. Coll., VI. 4th series, 325.

(3) Winthrop's Journal says: "Nov. 28, 1635. Here arrived a small Norsey bark of twenty-five tons sent by Lords Say &c., with one Gardiner an expert engineer or work base and provisions of all sorts to begin a fort at the mouth of Connecticut. She came through many great tempests; yet, through the Lord's great providence, her passengers twelve men and two women, and goods all safe."—Winthrop His. N. E., I, 173. The "Norsey bark," which for a long period puzzled Winthrop's annotators, was the "North Sea Boatt" Batcheler, referred to in Edward Hopkins' letter to John Winthrop, Jr. Vide Note (2)—C. C. G.

had set in unusnally early and was very severe, and, it is probable, that was the cause of his detention.

The authorities of Boston improved the opportunity of Gardiner's being there by engaging him to complete the fortifications on Fort Hill. At a town meeting held January 23rd, 1636, it was "agreed yt for ye raysing of a new worke of fortification vpon ye flort hill, about yt which is there alreaddy begune, the whole towne bestowe fourteéne dayes worke" a man. Commissioners were chosen, and a treasurer, and a "clarke"; and the work was to be commenced as soon as the weather would permit, for " ye engineere, Mr. Lyon Garner, who doth so freely offer his help therevnto, hath but a short time to stay."(1)

About the same time, the " Magistrates of the Bay" desired Gardiner to visit Salem, and "see how fit it was for fortification." He did so, and upon his return told them he thought the people were more in danger of starvation than of any "foreign potent enemy," and to defer works of that kind for the present. His own account of the affair concludes thus: "And they all liked my saying well."

Early in the spring Gardiner and his family continued their journey. The good ship *Bachelor* which had carried them safely from Holland to England and across the Atlantic was now to bear them to their destination.

### VI.—THE CONNECTICUT RIVER.

The valley of the Connecticut was early the object of acquisition. Its fertility, picturesque beauty and mild temperature attracted many from the seaboard settlements. To the Puritan emigrants it was the promised land. Four English plantations were commenced upon the river in the year 1635. A party from Watertown settled at Wethersfield; another party from Dorchester settled at Windsor; and another party from Cambridge settled at Hartford.

(1) NOTE.—In the margin of the town records are arranged in a column the following names, and against each is set £5; viz.: Bellingham, Vane, Winthrop, sen., Coddington, Winthrop, jun., Kayne, Hutchinson, Cogan, Leverett, and Harding.—S. G Drake's His. and Ant. of Boston, 188-89.

The fourth settlement was begun at the mouth of the river early in the month of November by a party of twenty men sent out by a bark from Boston under the direction of John Winthrop, the younger, who had recently returned from England (1) with a commission from the proprietaries of the territory at the mouth of the Connecticut to be Governor of the river and harbors and adjacent places for one year. Winthrop's commission instructed him to repair to the mouth of the Connecticut with all convenient speed and to provide at least fifty men to work at fortification and to build houses. First they were to erect houses for their own accommodation, after which they were ordered to construct others for "men of qualitie" which should be "within ye fort." The original projectors of this scheme of emigration were distinguished Lords and Gentlemen in England who had become thoroughly disgusted with the arbitrary government of Charles .the First. The names subscribed to Winthrop's commission, which was an agreement made in their "own names" and for the "rest of ye company," are the following: Lord Say and Seale, Sir Arthur Haslerigge, Sir Richard Saltonstall, Henry Lawrence, George Fenwick and Henry Darley Esq's. (2) It is known that Lord Brooke and Sir Matthew Boynton belonged to the company ; and Henry Vane, the younger, and Hugh Peters and others were active agents. There is little doubt but some of their number contemplated removing to the new plantation. (3) It is more than probable that

(1) Winthrop's Journal says: "Oct 6, 1635. There came also John Winthrop, the younger, with commission from the Lord Say, Lord Brooke and divers other great persons in England to begin a plantation at Connecticut and to be governor there. They sent also men and ammunition and £2,000 in money to begin a fortification at the mouth of the River."—Winthrop's His. N. E., 1, 170.

(2) Vide "Agreement of the Seabrook Company with John Winthrop, Jr."—Mass. Hist. Coll., 1, 5th series, 482.

(3) The following extracts of letters addressed to John Winthrop, Jr , by the parties named, will show something of their intent and interest in the Connecticut plantation at Saybrooke:
"Sir:    *    *    Our dependance on you is greate.    *    *    *    Your abilitie to performe your vndertaking we doubt not    *    *    *    only our request is that, with what speede possible may be, fitt houses be builded."    *    *    *    Sir A. Heslerigge and Geo. Fenwick.    Sep. 18. 1635.—Mass. Hist. Coll., VI, 4th series, 364.
"Sir:    *    *    *    I pray you advertise me what course I shall take for providinge a house against my cominge over, where I may remaine with my familie till I can be better provided to settle myself and lett me have your best assistance."    Sir Matt. Boynton.    Feb. 23. 1635.—Mass Hist. Coll., VII, 4th series, 164.
"Sir:    *    *    *    We are peremptory for Connecticut, it being, as you know, and so continuinge the joynte resolution of vs all, that nothing but a playne impossibility could divert us from that place    *    *    *    the time of your goinge up, when wee assuredly expect, shall be this winter    *    *    *    a third is, yt fortifications and some convenient buildinges for the receipt of gentlemen may go hande in hande, for there are like to come more over next summer    *    *    *    than you are yet aware of "    *    *    *    He: Lawrence. Sep. 22, 1635.—Mass. Hist. Coll , 1, 5th series, 215.
"Sir:    *    *    Sent you some servants, but not so many as we proposed.    *    *    *    Lord Brooke likewise, that vndertooke for XX tye failed and sent vs neil one. Our gentlemens minds remaine the same and are in a way of selling off their estates with the greatest expedition."    *    *    *    Philip Nye. Sep. 20 1635.—Mass. Hist. Coll. 1, 5th series, 213.

Lord Say and Seale, Sir Arthur Haslerigge, Sir Matthew Boynton and
Mr. Henry Lawrence intended to come.   One authority declares that
Lord Say and Lord Brooke were early in consultation with Hampden the kinsman of Cromwell.   Without doubt Hampden deemed it
prudent, at one time, to leave England; and, it is said, the two
cousins, Hampden and Cromwell, actually took passage in a vessel
which lay in the Thames bound for North America, when a royal
order prohibited the ship from sailing.  Seven other ships filled with
emigrants were stopped at the same time. (1)   "Hampden and
Cromwell remained, and with them remained the Evil Genius of
the House of Stuart." (2)

## VII.—SAYBROOKE FORT.

Winthrop's advance party, consisting of Lieutenant Gibbons,
Sergeant Willard, with some carpenters, took possession of a point
of land upon the west bank of the river, near its mouth, where there
was an excellent harbor, and began to fell trees and make a clearing,
late in November, 1635.  Very little progress was made towards a
settlement during the ensuing winter.  Probably a few log houses
were put up of the most primitive character.

The *Bachelor* arrived with Gardiner and family very early in the
following spring, probably in March.  The voyagers having reached
their destination, were doubtless rejoiced to step on firm earth, after
many months of tediousness and peril on the sea.  As compared
with the homes they had left what must have been their astonishment
at the view before them?  Let us hope that their first glances were
greeted with genial rays of sunshine, fresh verdure of budding trees,
and sweet fragrance of early blossoms.  The wild scene doubtless
suggested pleasures, yet it brought them anxieties.  A mere clearing
without habitable abodes, no fields for planting, and few laborers, was

(1) This story has been questioned, yet there is nothing improbable about it.  Hume, Hallam, Macaulay
and others relate it.   Arguments pro and con may be consulted in the N. E. Hist. and Gen. Register, 1861.
(2) Lord Macaulay's Essay on John Hampden.

10

not cheering for contemplation. Gardiner's account of the place at
their arrival shows considerable disappointment. He boldly asserts
that the company had not sent forward men "according to promise."
At least three hundred men were expected; some for fortification,
some for tilling the ground and others to build houses; but, the
"great expectation," Gardiner tauntingly remarks, came "only to
two men—Mr. Fenwick and his man." However, notwithstanding
every vexation and hindrance, the place was fortified by Gardiner
with the men and means at his command. A fort was constructed
of square-hewn timber with ditch, drawbridge, portcullis, rampart
and palisade. (1) This was the first fortification erected in New
England. (2) In honor of Lord Say and Seal and Lord Brooke, the
fort was named Saybrooke.

The Indians were more numerous in this vicinity than in any
other part of New England. The Pequots occupied both sides of the
Pequot River—now called the Thames—and numbered upwards of
seven hundred warriors; the Narragansetts and Mohegans were likewise formidable tribes; and all of them combined would make a
powerful enemy for the English to contend against, for at this time
the settlers on the Connecticut were very few in numbers; and in all
of the colonies not to exceed three hundred able men could be mus-
tered for duty. The dangers which threatened the settlements, threatened the fort. Besides hostile Indians, the Dutch of New Netherlands
lay in unfriendly proximity. However, the equanimity of the commander of the fort does not appear to have been disturbed by a
knowledge of his imperiled situation. Disappointments had been
met and could still be borne, and dangers were to be expected in the
possession of a fortified place.

On the 1st day of April, 1636, John Winthrop, Jr., arrived at the

(1) The following articles came as freight in the Bachelor; "Iron worke for 2 drawbridges, as follows:
62 staples, 40 staple hooks for portcullis, 4 chains, 10 boults, 4 plates, 8 chaine clasps, 4 under hinges, 23½ yards
of redd flagg stuffe for Serieant Gardener's vse & some small lines that came from Holland & a wheelbar-
row."—Mass. Hist. Coll., VI, 4th series, 326.
(2) History and traditions show that the fort was erected on a steep eminence which jutted out into
the river which was united to the main land by a sandy beach and was flanked by salt marshes. The land side of
the fort was protected by a palisade. It could not be successfully assailed by any near approaches of firm
ground. This fort was destroyed by fire in 1647.—C. C. G

fort.(1) He brought friendly messages for Gardiner. Sir Richard
Saltonstall, of Whitefreyers, England, wrote Winthrop: "Pray you
commend me, after yourselfe, to your good wife and Sergieant
Gardiner with his fellow soldier, whom I purpose, God willing, to
visitt this summer, if he will provide a house to recieue me and
mine att my landing."(2) Hugh Peters, then at Salem, wrote
Winthrop: "Salute honest Mr. Garddner and the rest."(3) And,
later in the month, William Pynchon, then at Roxbury, wrote
Winthrop: "I pray you remember my harty loue to Mr. Gardener
and the rest with you." (4) In the same month, Winthrop, the elder,
wrote his son: "Therefore I here end, with salutations to all our
friends, Mr. Gardiner, and his wife &c." (5) On May 16th, Winthrop
wrote his father that he had sent the *Bachelor* to Boston, but should
soon have use for her. On May 21st, Fenwick, one of the Saybrooke
Company, arrived at Boston and wrote Winthrop, that his coming
would not dissolve his commission. On June 23d, Winthrop, the
elder, wrote his son that the *Bachelor* would go back the next week ;
and that Fenwick, Peters, and some others would set out on horse-
back expecting to meet a shallop at one of the upper towns on
the Connecticut to take them down to the fort.(6)

Fenwick and Peters arrived at the fort early in July. They were
bearers of letters to Winthrop—one from his brother Adam closing

(1) John Winthrop, Jr., came on to Saybrooke fort from Boston, with his brother Stephen, perhaps,
and a small party, by land as far as Narragansett Bay, where they met the Indian Chief Canonicus, and
from thence by a vessel. He writes, in a letter to his father, from "Pasbeshauke," the Indian name for Saybrooke fort (a): dated "April 7, 1636." * * * " The first of this month we sett sayle from Narigansett,
and in the afternoone, about 4 a clocke, arrived heere; for this place I have not yet seene any thing that I
should be able to wright of it." * * Mass. Hist. Coll., VI, 4th series, 514-15. Winthrop's commission constituted him "Governor of the river Connecticut " * * one whole year after his arrival
there; " yet he appears to have entered upon his duties the previous autumn by sending men to locate and
prepare the place for settlement and fortification. Here began an official acquaintance between Gardiner and
Winthrop which soon ripened into a personal friendship that was continued with mutual confidence and
fidelity to the end of their lives.—C. C. G.
(a) The way this Indian name became known will be explained in the following letter, copied from
Mass. Hist. Society Proceedings, 1864-65, 475.
"Hartford, Sep. 20, 1855, Charles Deane, Esq., my dear sir: About PASBESHAUKE, the place where John
Winthrop, Jr., found himself on the 7th of April, 1636, and which neither of us could do more than hazard a
guess about when the first volume of the 'Winthrop Papers' was in press, I can now give you more exact
information. I have before me the original draft of a deed dated 'May 5, 1639,' by which 'YOYAWAN, Sachem
of Pommanoce, and ASWAW, Sachem his wife,' convey their ' Island called Manchonaut' to 'Lion Gardiner
commander of the forte called Saybrooke fort als PASHPESHAUKS at the mouth of the river of Kenecticut,'
* * * (Signed) J. H. TRUMBULL."
The "deed" referred to is in the hand-writing of Thos. Lechford, a lawyer of Boston from 1637 to 1641,
well known to students of colonial history, and will soon be published in the Lechford Record Book by the
American Antiquarian Society.—C. C. G. Also Vide Infra, p. 81, note (2).
(2) Mass. Hist. Coll., VI, 4th series, 581.          (3) Mass. Hist. Coll., VI, 4th series, 93.
(4) Mass. Hist. Coll., VI, 4th series, 379.          (5) Winthrop's Hist. N. E. I, 389.
(6) Winthrop's Hist. N. E., I, 392.

thus—"I pray remember my love to my brother Steven, and Mr. Gardnar and his wife, and all the rest of my friends;" (1) and another from his father, saying: "I paid Mr. Garsford of Salem £5 for a buff-coat for Mr. Gardiner, which you must remember to put to his account:" (2) also of a commission (3) from the Bay authorities requesting him to ask for a "solemn meeting of conference" with the Chief Sachem of the Pequots, and to demand of him the murderers of Capt. Stone and others; and, in case the demand was refused, to return the present (4)—a token of amity—which the Chief had sent the Bay authorities on a former occasion when a demand was made for the same murderers. Accordingly, Winthrop sent for Sassacus, and upon his arrival a conference was held, when the demand was made and refused; thereupon the present was returned, and immediately after Fenwick and Peters with Winthrop departed for Boston. (5) The return of the present was naturally construed into a declaration of war by the Pequots. Gardiner understood what would be its effect, and had endeavored to persuade the Bay authorities against their hot haste. He plead for delay and a more lenient policy until the new settlements grew stronger; but his entreaty availed nothing, the present was returned, said he "full sore against my will."

Immediately the Pequots began to plot against and irritate the neighboring settlements. Before the end of the month John Oldham, a well known trader, was killed by the Indians on Block Island. The Bay authorities charged the act upon the Pequots. Gardiner's account shows the murder was committed by the Narragansetts. The Bay authorities being undecided, were compelled to do something to satisfy the general clamor. "I wonder," said Gardiner, "that the Bay doth no better revenge the murdering

(1) Mass. Hist. Coll., VIII, 5th series, 259.   (2) Winthrop's Hist. N. E., 1, 391.
(3) Mass. Hist. Coll., III, 3d series, 129.
(4) The present consisted of "otter skin coats and beaver and skeins of wampum."—C. C. G.
(5) Winthrop did not return to the fort. He had been there just three months. His commission to be governor of the place was such that he could throw it up at any time. It is probable that his own projects demanded his attention elsewhere.—C. C. G.

of an honest man of their own?" Finally it was settled that the
Block Island Indians should be punished. An expedition was fitted
out, commanded by Endicott, which first landed at Block Island,
and then proceeded to the fort, "to my great grief," said Gardiner,
"for you come hither to raise these wasps about my ears and then
you will take wing and flee away." From thence the expedition
went to Pequot River. Gardiner, thinking there might be an opportunity for booty, sent along his shallop and another boat with twelve
men, and bags to fill with corn. He says his men "brought a pretty
quantity of corn" but the "Bay men killed not a man," only a
"Sachem of the Bay killed a Pequot;" and that began the war "in
these parts." The expedition was timid in action and unproductive
in results. · The authorities of Connecticut and of Plymouth thought
it ill-advised. It is evident that the ability of the Indians to make
reparation for offences was not well understood by the settlers. (1)

Immediately thereafter the fort was besieged by great numbers
of Indians lying in ambush; attacking all that ventured abroad;
killing, and sometimes roasting their victims alive. A trader named
Tilly landed on a point, in sight of the fort, and himself and another
man carelessly going on shore were captured and killed by the
Indians. Tilly was tortured in the most inhuman manner. Gardiner
had previously notified Tilly not to go ashore; and was given "ill
language" for his cautionary advice; so he called the place of Tilly's
rashness Tilly's Folly, now known as Tilly's Point. On the 22d of
February, 1637, Gardiner went out of the fort with ten men to burn
the reeds and leaves on a neck of land near the marsh. Suddenly
a "great company of Indians" came out of the woods from several
directions, while others sprang from the "fiery reeds," and all commenced a furious attack with their bows and arrows. Gardiner and
his party being largely out-numbered, began retreating and firing;
but they were closely pursued; even "on to the very muzzles of

(1) S. G. Drake's Hist. and Ant. of Boston, 202.

their pieces," so that at times they were compelled to defend themselves with their "naked swords." Gardiner was hit with many
arrows, one of which seriously wounded him in the thigh. Two of
his men were severely wounded, and four were shot dead. (1)   A few
days later the Pequots, thinking they had killed Gardiner in their
recent attack upon him, swarmed about the fort fully three hundred strong.   Their attitude showed they were bent upon mischief.
Gardiner called for his "sword, pistols, and carbine," and ordered
out a small party for a parley.   At first the Pequots did not know
Gardiner, for, said they, he was shot with many arrows; and "so I
was," said Gardiner, "but my buff-coat preserved me, and only one
hurt me;" (2) but when he spake they knew his voice, and began to
fall back.   At the close of the parley he gave a signal to his gunner
at the fort, and "the two great guns went off" which caused a "great
hubbub amongst them" and made them beat a speedy retreat.

Late in March, Governor Vane sent a messenger with a letter to
Gardiner requesting him to "prescribe the best way to quell the
Pequots."   In his reply, Gardiner "presumed to send an arrow,"
that had killed one of his men, "with the head sticking fast half
through the man's rib-bone"—as a token—because it was reported
at the Bay that Indian arrows had no force. (3)   About the 10th of
April, Underhill arrived with twenty lusty men from the Bay.   They
came upon the requisition of Gardiner and were to remain "till
something should be done about the Pequots."

While the colonists were debating upon the gravity of the
situation a massacre was committed by the Pequots near Wethersfield — fourteen men and women were killed, and two maids were
carried away. (4)   The maids were soon liberated by some Dutch

(1) MATHER says there were about seventy Indians who fought Gardiner, and that they killed four of his
men; that a fifth who was sorely wounded recovered, and lived to cut off the head of the very Indian who
shot him, the next year.—S. G. Drake's Hist. and Ant. of Boston, 205.

(2) The English soldiers armor at that time was a steel cap and corselet with back and breast pieces over
buff coats.—C. C. G.

(3) Extract from a letter of Ed. Winslow of Plymouth to John Winthrop, the elder    "Mr. Gardiner, it
seems, much discourageth common men by extolling the valor of your adversaries, preferring them before the
Spaniards."—Mass. Hist. Coll., VI, 4th series, 164.

(4) April 23, 1637

traders who went in a sloop to Pequot River, and secured them
by a resort to stratagem. Gardiner says he sent the Dutchmen
at his own cost who returned the maids to the fort almost naked,
whom he clothed and sent home.

At a general court held at Hartford, (1) it was voted to raise
ninety men, and make an attack on the Pequots stronghold beyond
Pequot River. The Bay authorities, through the efforts of Roger
Williams, effected a secret alliance with Miantonomoh, Chief of the
Narragansetts; and the Connecticut settlers secured Uncas, Chief of
Mohegans, who had rebelled against the authority of Sassacus, and
naturally attached himself to the settlers for protection and for
revenge. The Pequots now stood alone and defiant! In a few days
Mason with ninety settlers, and Uncas with eighty warriors dropped
down the river to the fort, from whence the combined forces were to
move. To Mason, Gardiner and Underhill was given full authority
to fit out the expedition. Gardiner says "we old soldiers agreed
about the way." Mason held the chief of command. Twenty "insufficient men" were sent home and their places were filled by an
equal number of the "lustiest" at the fort. The friendship of Uncas
was satisfactorily tested by a novel plan proposed by Gardiner, and
a surgeon, and provisions were supplied by the fort—and the brave
little army sailed out of the Connecticut. (2)

Our subject does not require a further statement of particulars.
Colonial historians have related the story of the encounter. In
one brief hour the proud Pequots were nearly exterminated and
the victorious colonists hastened to their homes. Mason and about
twenty of his men returned across the country; arriving at the shore
opposite to the fort at sunset. Gardiner "observed his approach;
and never did the heart of a Roman consul, returning in triumph,
swell more than the pride of Mason and his friends, when they found
themselves received as victors; and 'nobly entertained with many

(1) May 1, 1637.
(2) The attack was made on the Pequot fortress at Mistick on the morning of May 26th, 1637.—C. C. G.

great guns.'"(1)    On the following morning Mason and his party
crossed the river and received "many courtesies" from the commander of the fort. (2)

The fall of the Pequots put an end to Indian depredations; and
the prospect of an enduring peace brought increased prosperity to
the river settlements.   The fort was maintained at its former strength;
the commander was watchful, but a warlike vigilance was not
required; he could now practice husbandry without the aid of
"great guns," and hold a parley without calling for his "sword,
pistols and carbine."

The Narragansetts were now the most powerful of the tribes
in this vicinity, and promptly asserted their supremacy by de-
manding tribute from their neighbors.   The Montauks declined
to acknowledge their power, preferring the friendship of the settlers, and Wyandanch, Sachem of the Montauks, came to the fort to
ask for peace and trade with the settlers promising to pay tribute
in wampum.   Gardiner granted his request, and assured him of
friendship and protection so long as his tribe kept their pledges to
the English.   Such was the situation of affairs when the engagement
of Commander Gardiner with the Saybrooke Company expired, which
was in the summer of 1639.

Lion Gardiner's life and experiences at Saybrooke Fort would
not be entirely complete without stating that his newly married wife,
with her maid, was an occupant of the fort and shared with him its
deprivations and dangers and bore him two children, first, David,
born April 29th 1636; and, second, Mary,(3) born August 30th, 1638.
David was the first child born of English parents in Connecticut.

(1) Bancroft's Hist. of the U. S. Vol. I. 467.
(2) Vide Mason's History of the Pequot war.—Mass. Hist. Coll., VIII, 2nd series, 120-132.
(3) This daughter married Jeremiah Conkling of East Hampton, L. I., ancestor of the Conkling family
of New York—notably Judge Alfred Conkling and his sons Hon. Roscoe Conkling and Col. Fred'k A. Conkling.

## VIII.—MANCHONACK *alias* ISLE OF WIGHT.

Gardiner early comprehended the situation of affairs at Say-brooke and wrote Winthrop, soon after the latter departed from the fort, saying: "it seemes wee have neather masters nor owners;" at the same time, said he, "there shall be noe cause to complayne of our flidelitie and endeavours to you ward;" yet, if not provided for, "then must I be fforced to shift as the Lord may direct."(1)

Notwithstanding every discouragement Gardiner remained at his post and fulfilled his contract to the end; and, when "fforced to shift," was fortunate in securing from the Indians the possession of a large island in Long Island Sound, called by them *Manchonack*, signifying, by tradition, "a place where many had died." The original deed of purchase bears date May 3, 1639, by which " *Yovawan*, Sachem of Pommanoce, and *Aswaw*, his wife," convey their "Island called Manchonat" to " *Lion Gardiner*, commander of the forte called Saybrooke fort als Pashpeshanks, at the mouth of the river of Kennecticot."(2) According to tradition the consideration paid was " one large black dog, one gun, a quantity of powder and shot, some rum and a few Dutch blankets."(3) Subsequently Gardiner procured a grant of the same island, called by the English *Isle of Wight*, from an agent of

(1) Vide Supra, pp. 35-36.

(2) Vide Supra, p. 75, note (a). Also, the following :—C. C. G.

HARTFORD, August 15, 1861.

Mr. C. C. GARDINER, St. Louis, Mo., Dear Sir: I send you a copy of the Deed of Gardiner's Island. The uniform tradition of the purchase from Walandance is, as you will see, unfounded. Walandance, as Gardiner mentions in his narrative, was a younger "brother of the old Sachem of Long Island," who "dwelt at Shelter Island," and was not, at the date of this deed, himself, Sachem. Pommanoce was an Indian name of Long Island—or rather of the east end of the Island. Yovawau, the old Sachem, may have been the elder brother of Walandance, who was called by the English, Poggatacut. See Prime's History of L. I., p. 91.

Yours Truly, (Signed) J. HAMMOND TRUMBULL.

INDIAN DEED OF GARDINER'S ISLAND: " Knowe all men by these presents, that we YOVAWAN Sachem of Pommanoce and ASWAW his wife for ten coats of trading cloath to us before the making hereof payed and delivered by LION GARDINER commander of the forte called Saybrooke fort als Pashpeshanks at the mouth of the River of Kennecticot, doe hereby for us and our heirs and successors grant, bargaine and sell unto the said LION GARDINER all that our Island called Manchonat with the appurtenances and all our right, title and demand of, in and to the same, to have and to hold the said Island with the appurtenances unto the said LION GARDINER his heirs and assignes forever. IN WITNESS whereof we have hereto sett our hands and seales the third day of the month, called, by the English, May in the yeare by them of their Lord written one thousand six hundred thirty and nine, 1639."

[Signatures and seals not given in copy.]

From the original draft by Thomas Lechford.—J. H. TRUMBULL.

(3) This tradition is not well founded, as will be seen by reading the Indian Deed.—C. C. G.

11

Earl of Stirling, grantee of the King of England, (1) bearing date March 10, 1639 [o. s.] (2)

He removed with his family to his island soon after purchasing it of the Indians, taking with him a number of men from the fort for farmers—forming, it is said, the earliest English settlement within the present limits of the State of New York. The island was then a wilderness, far away from European settlements and open to Indian depredations; but, without doubt, was guarded by Gardiner's trusted friend Wyandanch, Sachem of the Montauks, between whom and himself there appears to have existed a remarkably close and firm friendship—a Heathen and Christian—that continued steadfast and unbroken even unto death!

In 1641, Gardiner's daughter Elizabeth was born on the 14th day of September—the first birth from English parents in the Province of New York.

In 1642, Miantonomoh visited the Montauks and endeavored to persuade them to give wampum to the Narragansetts, and not to the English. Gardiner, happening to be with the Montauks, advised Wyandanch not to give any answer, but to ask for a month's delay to consider the subject. Meantime Gardiner wrote of the matter by Wyandanch to Gov. Haines at Hartford, who forbade the Montauks

(1) COPY OF EARL OF STIRLING'S GRANT TO LION GARDINER.—Know all whom this present Writing may concern, that I, James Farrett of Long Island, Gent. Deputy to the Right Hon'ble the Earll of Starling Secretary for the Kingdom of Scotland, doe by these presents, in the name and behalf of the said Earll of Starling and in my own name also, as his Deputy, as I doth or may concern myself, Give & Grant free leave and liberty to Lion Gardiner his heirs, executors and assigns to enjoy that Island which he hath now in possession called by the Indians Manchonack, by the English the Isle of Wight; I say to enjoy both now & for ever, which Island hath been purchased, before my coming, from the ancient Inhabitants, the Indians; Nevertheless though the said Lion Gardiner had his possession first from the Indians before my coming, yet is he now contented to hold the tenor & title of the possession of the aforesaid Island from the Earll of Starling or his successors whomsoever, who hath a Grant from the King of England, under the Great Seal of the aforesaid Kingdom. Bee it known, therefore, that I, the said James Farrett doe give & hath given free liberty and power to the said Lion Gardiner, his Heirs, Exe'rs and Assigns and their Successors for ever to enjoy the possession of the aforesaid Island, to build & plant thereon as best liketh them, and to dispose thereof as they think fitt, and also to make, execute & put in practice such laws for Church and Civil Government as are according to God, the Kings and the practise of the Country, without giving any account thereof to any whomsoever and the aforesaid Right & title, both of land and Government to remayne with, and to them and their successors for ever, without any trouble or molestation from the said Earll or any of his successors, for now & forever. And as much as it hath pleased Our Royal King to give the Patten of Long Island to the aforesaid Earle of Starling in consideration whereof it is agreed upon that the trade with the Indians shall remayne with, the said Earle and his successors, to dispose upon from time to time and at all times as best liketh him. Notwithstanding (allowing) the said Lion Gardiner to trade with the Indyans for Corne or any Kinde of victuals for the use of the Plantation and no farther; and if the said Lion Gardiner shall trade in Wampum from the Indyans hee shall pay for every (adome twenty shillings and also the said Lion Gardiner and his successors shall pay to the said Earle or his deputyes a yearly acknowledgment being the sum of Five Pounds, (being lawfully demanded) of lawfull money of England, or such commoditys as at that time shall pass for money in the country; and the first payment to begin on the last of Oct. 1643, the three former years being advanced for the use of the said James Farrett. In witness whereof the party has put his hands and seal the tenth day of March 1639        [o. s.]
(Signed)    JAMES FARRETT    (seal.)

Sealed and delivered in the presence of Balk Davis, Benju Price.
(2) According to New Style, this date should be reckoned as March 10, 1640.

giving wampum to the Narragansetts. The next year, Miantonomoh visited the Montauks, bringing them gifts; and, Wyandanch being absent, he held a secret consultation with the old men of the tribe. On Wyandanch's return he was told of the secret talk and carried the news to Gardiner, who notified Gov. Eaton at New Haven and Gov. Haines at Hartford—so Miantonomoh's second attempt failed. After the death of Miantonomoh, his successor, Ninigret, sent one of his chief men to the Montauks to form an alliance against the English, and Wyandanch seized and bound him and turned him over to Gardiner, who sent him under guard with a letter to Gov. Eaton at New Haven. Being wind bound at Shelter Island, he got away from the guard in the night and returned to his tribe. This was another of the plots of the Narragansetts which was discovered, and revealed to the English, by the faithful Wyandanch.

Previous to the Peqnot war a giant-like Indian, toward the west, killed a man named Hammond, in Southampton, and he could not be taken because he was protected by Poggatacut, Sachem of Manhasset. Afterwards the same Indian killed another man named Farrington—yet he could not be found. Wyandanch sought out the murderer after the death of Poggatacut and killed him by the direction of Gardiner. Then, a woman was killed, by some unknown Indians, and the magistrates sent for Wyandanch to appear and produce the murderers, but his tribe being fearful of his safety would not let him go. Wyandanch then said, "I will hear what my friend will say"—meaning Gardiner, who, being there, saw the difficulty, and offered himself as a hostage for the safe return of Wyandanch, and was accepted, with loud and joyous shouts of thanks from the tribe. That same night Wyandanch departed, with a note from Gardiner saying that no one should "stay him" but to "let him eat and drink and be gone," and before his return he found four "consenters" to the murder, who were arrested and afterwards hung at Hartford—one of whom was the Blue Sachem. The foregoing instances are related to show that Wyandanch was the faithful friend of the settlers, even when murders were committed by the Long Island Indians.

In 1649, Gardiner became one of the original purchasers of about 30,000 acres of land for the settlement at East Hampton, which was first called Maidstone. In 1650, the first church was gathered at East Hampton. The same year Gardiner wrote John Winthrop, Jr., about a young man, not named, for a minister—it may have been Thomas James. (1)

In 1651, Poggatacut, Sachem of Manhasset, died, and his brother, Wyandanch, succeeded him as Grand Sachem of Paumanacke, as Long Island was called by the Indians.

In 1653, Gardiner placed his island in the care of farmers and removed with his family to East Hampton. (2) His place of residence was on the east side of the main street, toward the southern extremity of the town, nearly opposite to the old burying ground in which it is supposed himself and wife and some of his descendants were buried. The same place is now owned by a descendant.

In 1654, a war broke out between the Narragansetts and Montauks. Frequent incursions were made by both tribes. On a certain raid upon the Montauks, by Ninigret he captured the daughter of Wyandanch on the night of her nuptials and killed her sponse, and captured and killed many others. Through the exertions of Gardiner the hapless bride was redeemed and restored to her afflicted parents. In grateful remembrance, Wyandanch presented his friend Gardiner a free gift of land, by deed bearing date July 14, 1659, comprising the principal part of the present town of Smithtown, L. I. (3) In 1655, and likewise in 1657, Gardiner, with others,

---

(1) Vide supra, p. 6.

(2) Joshua Garlicke, Benjamin Price and John Miller, were at different times overseers of the island.— Ch. of E. Hampton.

(3) Office Secretary of State, Albany, N. Y., Book of Deeds, Vol. II, p. 118, "East-Hampton, July 14th, 1659. Be it known unto all men, both English and Indyans, especially the inhabitants of Long Island, That I, Wyandance, Sachem of Paumanuck, with my wife and sonne Wyankanbone, my only sonne and heire, having deliberately considered, how this Twenty-foure yeare wee have been not only acquainted with Lyon Gardiner, but from time to time have received much kindnesse of him, and from him not only by Counnell and advice, in our prosperity, but in our great extremity, when wee were almost swallowed up of our enemyes, then wee say hee appeared to us, not only as a friend, but as a father, in giving us of his money and goods, whereby wee defended ourselves, and ransomed my Daughter and friends. And wee say and know, that by his meanes, we had great comfort and reliefe, from the most Honobl of the English Nation here about us, so that seeing wee yet live, an-l both of us being now old, and not that we at any time have given him any thing to gratify his

were appointed a committee to visit Hartford and treat with the magistracy about placing East Hampton under the protection of Connecticut.

In 1657, Goody Garlicke, wife of Joshua Garlicke of East Hampton, was charged with witch-craft. Witnesses deposed many facts and much debate arose. Gardiner charged one witness with falsification and declared the accused innocent. Her case was referred to the general court at Hartford, but she was never taken there and the matter was not heard of afterwards.

In 1658, Gardiner became one of the purchasers in the original conveyance from the Indians of about 9,000 acres of land on Montauk Point. (1) The grantees guaranteed protection to the Montauks, and the latter reserved the right to live on the lands—a right their posterity have ever since enjoyed. In the same year Wyandanch brought a suit against one Daily, for damage done his "great cannow," which was tried by three men. Gardiner testified in the case, and the jury found for the plaintiff ten shillings damages and court charges. (2) In the same year, a fatal epidemic spread among the Montauks and destroyed more than half of the tribe. Wyandanch died, that year, by poison secretly administered. Previous to his death he appointed Gardiner and his son David guardians to his son Wyancombone, who, it appears, divided the government of his tribe with his widowed mother, styled Sunk-Squa—meaning something like Dowager-Queen. Gardiner pathetically remarks upon the death

love, care and Charge, wee having left that is worth his acceptance, but a small Tract of land and we desire him to accept it for himselfe, his heires, Executors and Assignes for ever: Nowe that it may bee knowne how, and where this Land lyeth on Long Island, We say it lyeth between Huntington and Seatalcott the westerne Bounds being Cowharbour, Easterly Ashamomuck, and Southerly crosse ye island to the end of ye great hollow or valley or more than halfe through the Island, and that this is our free Act and Deed, doth appeare by our hand Markes underwritten, Signed, sealed and delivered in the presence of Richard Smith, Thomas Chatfield, Thomas Talmage, by Wyandance, his mark. Wyankanbone, his mark. Sachem's wife, her mark."

On the same page follows immediately the following entry: "Moreover, I, Wyankanbone with my Mother do acknowledge to have sold to Lyon Gardiner above-named, the next jacent Tract of Land Easterly, That is to say, Nesequake River, and all the land both Neck and Creekes, thereunto belonging, and to runne parulel through the Island with the other, and have reed so much for it, as wee demanded, to our full content, so that that land from Cowharbour to Nesaquake River with the same River, belongeth to Lyon Gardiner his heires, Executors and Assigns forever. This done by us this 6th of April 1660. Witness our hands Markes & scales to ye puts of these, wee say not only the Land, but all yt doth or shall naturally grow thereon.—Thomas Talmage, Thomas Chatfield, by Wyankanbone, his mark. His mother, her mark. Achemanus, a witnesse."

I copied the above from Albany Correspondence in the SIGNAL of Babylon, L. I., June 30, 1883.—C. C. G.

(1) The purchase was confirmed by deed August 1, 1660, and Feb. 11, 1661.—C. C. G.

(2) Hedges' Two Hundredth Anniversary Address, East Hampton, 1849.

of Wyandanch. "my friend and brother is gone, who will now do the like?"(1)   In the same year, Gardiner made his Will.(2)

In 1659, Gardiner was prosecuted, before the magistrates of East Hampton, by certain English captors of a Dutch vessel, for retaking the Dutch vessel at his island; damages were laid at £500.  The case was referred to the general court at Hartford, but was never tried.(3)

In 1660, Gardiner wrote his well known and often quoted "Relation of the Pequot Wars."(4)

In 1662, Gardiner, with others, were chosen to "compound a difference," between certain parties, "about Meantaquit."

In the same year Gardiner's daughter Elizabeth, wife of Arthur Howell, died leaving a daughter Elizabeth.

In 1663, Gardiner conveyed his lands in Smithtown, L. I., to Richard Smith of R. I., whom he had known when at Saybrooke.

In the latter part of 1663, Gardiner died at the age of 64.   In 1664 his widow made her Will,(5) and early in 1665 she died at the age of 64.   Both were buried at East Hampton.

---

(1) Vide Supra, p. 30.

(2) WILL OF LION GARDINER.—Be it known to all men by these presents that I, Lion Gardiner of Easthampton, do by these make my last Will and Testament, first then I give, bequeath my soul to God that gave it, my body to the earth from whence it came, my estate as followeth.  First, then I leave my wife, Mary, whole and sole executor and administrator of all that is, or may be called mine, only whereas, my daughter, Elizabeth, hath had ten head of cattle, so I will that my son David, and my daughter Mary shall each of them have the like.  As for my whole estate, both the Island and that I have at Easthampton, I give it to my wife, that she may dispose of it before her death as God shall put it into her mind; only this I put into her mind, of that, whereas, my son David after he was at liberty to provide for himself by his own engagements, hath forced me to part with a great part of my estate to save his credit, so that at present, I cannot give to my daughter and grand-child that which is fitting for them to have, but I leave it to my wife with the overseers of my will to give to each of them as God shall put into her mind that she will, and dispose of all as she will, and the cause that moves me at present to make this Will, is not only the premises, but other causes known to me and my wife, of whom and for whom I stand, and am bound to provide and take care for so long as I live, so that when I am dead, by wilful neglect she be not brought to poverty which might be a cause to her of great grief and sorrow.  The executors of this my Will, I desire to be Mr. Thomas James, the Reverend Minister of the Word of God at Easthampton, with John Mulford and Robert Bond, whom I will that they shall have for every day spent about this my Will; I say they shall have five shillings for every day each of them and their charges borne.  But in case that three of the overseers of my Will should not be then here, two or one will my wife may choose others.  Witness my own hand seal the 13th August, 1658.

(Signed)        LION GARDINER.

Witness: Thomas James.   The within writing is a true copy of Mr. Lion Gardiner, his Will as it was produced unto and approved by the Court here at Southampton, and by the said Court ordered to be recorded by me, Henry Pierson, Register.   Will and Inventory of property recorded in a book entitled, Town and County Records, Liber A., page 18 and 19, [1663] deposited among the town records of Southampton. (Long Island, N. Y.)

(3) Vide Supra, p. 46.

(4) Vide Supra, p. 14, et seq.

(5) WILL OF MARY GARDINER, WIDOW OF LION GARDINER.—Be it known unto all men by these presents that I, Mary Gardiner of Maidstone, als Easthampton upon Long Island, being in good and perfect understanding, I say I do by these presents make my last Will and Testament.  I. I bequeath my soul to God, and my body to the earth from whence it came, and mine estate as followeth: I give my Island, called the Isle of Wight (alias Monchonock) to my son David, wholly to be his during his life, and after his decease, to his next heire malle begotten by him, then my Will is, it shall succeed to the heire malle of my daughter Mary, as an Inheritance; and if she die without an heire malle, to succeed to the heire malle of my grand-child Elizabeth, and to be entayled to the first heires malle proceeding from the body of my deceased husband, Lion Gardiner, and me his wife Mary, from time to time, forever.  Never to be sold from them but to be a continuous inheritance to the heires of me and my husband forever; but if in future time the heires malle shall be extinct, then to succeed to the females in an equall division as shall be found most

Thus passed from earth one of the prominent figures in the early colonial history of New England.

Lion Gardiner was singularly modest; firm in his friendships; "patient of toil; serene amidst alarms; inflexible in faith"—and he "died in a good old age, an old man and full of years."

just and equall for the dividing the said Island. II. I give to my daughter Mary, my whole accommodations at Easthampton or Maidstone with all the housing and privileges appertaining to the same. III. I give the one-halfe of my stock, viz., neat kinde, horse kinde and sheepe, the one-halfe I say I give to my daughter Mary to be divided equally by my overseers of this my Testament. IV. I give the one-halfe of all my house-hold goods to my daughter Mary, to be divided by my overseers in equall parts. V. I give the other halfe of my stock to my grand-child, both that which is at the Island or elsewhere, to be divided as aforesaid. VI. I give the other halfe of my household goods to my grand-child Elizabeth, to be divided as aforesaid, but with this proviso, I give my stock and household goods, the one part as aforesaid to my grand-childe Elizabeth; if God be pleased to continue her to the age of fifteen years, then to be delivered to her by mine executors whom I appoint to be my son David. A just account being taken by my overseers both of the stock and household goods after my decease: But if she, my said grand-childe die before the age of fifteen yeares, or before shee be maryed, then the aforesaid stock and goods shall be equally divisted, and the one part my son David shall have, and the other my daughter Mary or their heires. I will also that if my son David please he shall have the keeping of the stock and goods, till my foresaid grande-childe come to the age aforesaid, he giving suf-ficient security to the overseers of this my Will and Testament, both of the cattle and goods fall to the share of my said grande-childe. But if my son David shall refuse this, then my son-in-law to have the refusal, but if both refuse, then my Will is, that my overseers take the best way they can for the security of the said estate bequeathed by me to my grande-childe Elizabeth. The overseers of this my Will and Testament I desire to be Mr. Thomas James, Minister of the Word of God, and Mr. John Mulford, Mr. Robert Bond, all of Easthampton. And what time they shall spend within here on the Island, about this my Will, I allow them the same as formerly my husband Lion deceased, in his last Will and Testament hath appointed them; but if any one shall be deceased or removed, then any two of them that remaine to do the worke as if all three were present, if two be absent of these of the overseers as aforesaid, then hee that remaines to take or choose one or two more with him and with consent of my heires to be allowed as aforesaid. Lastly: My will is, my two servants Japhet and Roose, my son David shall have the one, and my daughter Mary the other, my son David choosing which of them he will have. VII. Know also, and this be understood, that there is a bill of twenty-five pounds left in my hands by my husband, Lion Gardiner; this bill shall be discharged to my son-in-law Arthur, or his heires, if my grande-childe should dye before shee come to the age aforesaid; this bill I will to be discharged by my son David and "Jeremiah," and they both to part the goods between them, for which that bill was made.

For confirmation of this my Will and Testament, I set to my hand and seale (signed) MARY GARDINER. Witnesse: Thomas James, John Mulford, Robert Bond; April 19th, 1664. Memorandum: I, Mary Gardiner, upon good consideration since this my Will and Testament was made, do in all respects confirm the same, saving or excepting the horse kinde upon the Island, my last Will being to give to the children of my son David, and daughter Mary, my grande-children, all the horse kinde between them to be equally divided and improved for their best advantage till they come of age. Witnesse my hand.                    (Signed) MARY GARDINER.

Witnesse: John Mulford, Robert Bond, Thomas James. The probation of this Will, the 6th of June, [1665] before ye Court of Sessions held in Southold, was attested upon oath by two of the witnesses, namely: Thomas James, John Mulford.

NOTE.

Lion Gardiner was at an early age a God-fearing Puritan; he emigrated in the interest of Puritanism, and labored with and for the early fathers, and justly belongs among the founders of New England. After leaving Saybrooke he was still, practically, under New England protection both at his Island and at East Hampton. All of his social, religious and trade relations were with the settlers of New England. His Island was an independent plantation during his life time, and East Hampton and the other towns at the east end of Long Island were during the same period under the protection of Connecticut until 1662. At no time was he ever called upon to recognize the government of New York. His son David first acknowledged the suprem-acy of the government of New York in 1665.—C. C. G.

# EDITORIAL EGOTISM.

# EDITORIAL EGOTISM.

FINIS CORONAT OPUS.

*Thirty years ago I began a search for my ancestry, a pursuit I thoroughly enjoyed, as a pastime, because it brought me many entertaining letters, with fresh facts and interesting reminiscences. Within a comparatively brief period I was the possessor of a mass of materials sufficient to make a moderate volume, yet I had no thought of preparing the matter for publication. I was content to rest from my labors, when I had succeeded in establishing a complete chain of descent from my earliest ancestor in this country.*

*Here is my pedigree: Curtiss Crane Gardiner, born in Eaton, N. Y., December 1, 1822; the son of Lyman Gardiner, born in Sherburne, N. Y., July 25, 1798, married first Mary Crane, died at Nunda, N. Y., December 7, 1846; the son of Daniel Denison Gardiner, born in Groton, Ct., March 28, 1773, married Eunice Otis, died at Eaton, N. Y., July 17, 1817; the son of William Gardiner, born in Groton, Ct., September 5, 1741, married Esther Denison, died at Chenango Forks, N. Y., March 31, 1800; the son of Joseph Gardiner, born on Gardiner's Island, April 22, 1697, married Sarah Grant, died at Groton, Ct., May 15, 1752; the son of John Gardiner, born on Gardiner's Island, April 19, 1661, married first Mary King, died at New London, Ct., June 25, 1738; the son of David Gardiner, born in Saybrooke Fort, Ct., April 29, 1636, married Mary Heringman,*      *Herringham.* *widow, died at Hartford, Ct., July 10, 1689; the son of Lion Gardiner, the progenitor of the family in America.*

*I then gathered up the letters and papers which had accumulated in the course of my search, and carefully packed them away, and they remained packed away in my possession, from 1855 to 1882—twenty-seven years—when I found it necessary to consult them as aids in the preparation of the manuscript for this volume. Unfolding those old, familiar letters—companions of other days—I discovered the Great Destroyer of all living had cut down all but one of the writers. Such a destruction was appalling and well calculated to awaken the most solemn reflections. But such is life. True, my old friends had passed away, yet I found consolation in the fact that they had left me valuable autograph letters; and what is so like one's friend as his letters? In one instance, a letter which I had written to one of those old correspondents, became the subject of a conspicuous newspaper item, in the following language: "There is a letter in the post office at S—— S——, (N. Y.), addressed to Mr. G——r V——W——k. As that gentleman has slept with his forefathers nearly a quarter of a century, we are not a little curious to know who it is that has for so many years survived him, and not yet learned that he long ago wrapped 'the drapery of his couch about him and lies down to pleasant dreams.'" My experience reminded me of Rip Van Winkle, when he returned to his native village, after twenty years' sleep in the Highlands. Like him, I found my old friends "gone," and like him I was ready, for the moment, to doubt my own existence, and to exclaim "I'm not myself—I'm some body else."*

*The production of this volume should be credited to the publication of the "Winthrop Papers." It appeared to me, after reading that valuable collection, that if some one should make a compilation of all the papers of Lion Gardiner, such a volume would be an acceptable offering to his descendants. If I have succeeded in that, my purpose has been fulfilled.*

*All of the authorities consulted have been credited in the proper places, except where the same events have appeared in a number of publications without any claim to originality. All histories of the* early colonial times in *New England*, and of the *Eastern settlements of Long Island*, necessarily mention *Lion Gardiner*. A memoir of him, by *Alexander Gardiner*, was published in 1849, by the *Massachusetts Historical Society, Vol. X, 3d Series, pp. 173–185.* His career is referred to very fully in the "*Two-Hundredth Anniversary*" Address, by *H. P. Hedges*, at *East Hampton*, published in 1850. He is likewise written up exhaustively in the "*Chronicles of East Hampton*," by *David Gardiner*, published in 1871. The "*History of the City of New York*," by *Mrs. M. J. Lamb*, refers to him, but is more devoted to his descendants.

My acknowledgments are due to a number of gentlemen, and to one lady, none of whom I have the pleasure to know, and I do not feel authorized to mention their names. With grateful remembrances to all, I beg to say that I have found them agreeable, painstaking and obliging correspondents, and I hope they may never have cause to regret having contributed, what they could, to this work. Only a limited edition will be printed, solely for private circulation. Dated this 27th day of August, 1883.

# APPENDIX.

possession, they gave a receipt—the original of which is still preserved by the family, as follows: (1)

BOSTON, NEW-ENGLAND, July, 25, 1699.

A true account of all such gold, silver, jewels, and merchandise, late in the possession of Captain William Kidd, which have been seized and secured by us under written pursuant to an order from his Excellency Richard Earl of Bellomont, Captain General and Governor in Chief in and over her Majesty's Province of the Massachusetts Bay, &c. bearing date July 7, 1699.

In Capt. Wm. Kidd's box, viz.

| | ounces |
|---|---|
| One bag qt fifty-three silver bars | 357 |
| One bag qt seventy-nine bars and pieces of **silver** | 442½ |
| One bag qt seventy-four bars of silver | 421 |

One enameled silver box guilt in which are—four diamonds set **in gold lockets**, one diamond loose, one large diamond set in a gold ring.

Found in the Mr. Duncan Campbell's house:

| | | ounces |
|---|---|---|
| No. 1. | one bag qt of gold | 58½ |
| 2. | one bag qt | 94 |
| 3. | one handkerchief qt | 50 |
| 4. | one bag qt | 103 |
| 5. | one bag qt | 38½ |
| 6. | one bag qt | 19½ |
| 7. | one bag qt of silver | 203 |

**Also** twenty dollars one-half and one-quarter pieces of eight, nine English Crowns, one small bar of silver, one small lump of silver, a small chain, a small bottle, a coral necklace, one piece of white and one piece of chequered silk.

In Capt. Wm. Kidd's chest, viz: two silver casons, two silver candlesticks, one silver porringer, and some small things of silver qt 82 ounces. Rubies small and great, sixty-seven green stones—69 precious stones. One large load stone.

Landed from on board the sloop Antonia, Capt. Wm. Kidd late **commander**, 57 bales of sugar, 17 canvass pieces, 41 bales of merchandise.

Received of Mr. Duncan Campbell three bales of merchandise, whereof one he had opened being much dammified by water qt—— eighty-five pieces of silk Ronralls and Bangalls. Sixty pieces of calico and muslins.

Received the 17th instant of Mr John Gardiner, **viz:**

| | | ounces. |
|---|---|---|
| No. 1. | **one** bag dust gold qt | 603¼ |
| 2. | one bag coyned gold qt | 11 |
| | and in it silver qt | 124 |
| 3. | one bag dust gold qt | 24¾ |
| 4. | one bag qt three silver rings and sundry **precious stones** | 4⅜ |
| | one bag unpolished stones qt | 12½ |
| | one pure crystal and brazer stones two Cornelian rings, two small agates, two amethysts, all in the same bag. | |
| 5. | one bag silver buttons and a lamp | 29 |
| 6. | **one** bag broken silver qt | 173½ |
| 7. | **one** bag gold bars | 353¼ |
| 8. | **one** bag gold bars | 238½ |
| 9. | **one** bag dust gold | 59½ |
| 10. | one bag silver bars | 212 |
| 11. | one bag silver bars | 309 |

The whole of the gold above mentioned is eleven hundred and eleven ounces Troy **Wt.** The silver is two thousand three hundred and fifty-three ounces.

The jewels or precious stones weighed—are seventeen ounces three-eighths of an ounce and sixty-nine stones by scale.

The sugar is contained in 57 bags. **The merchandise contained in 41 bales. The** canvass in seventeen pieces.

(1) I made this copy from the **original document at the Island, August 9th and 10th, 1855.**—C. C. G.

A true account of the first sheet of the accompt of the treasure goods and merchandise imported by Captain William Kidd and company and accomplices Anno 1699. Seized by order of the Earl of Bellomont which accompt was presented in thirteen sheets under the hands of Samuel Sewall, Nathaniel Byfield, Jeremiah Dumer, and Andrew Belcher, Esq., Commissioners appointed to receive and secure and upon their oaths.—And is lodged in the Secretary's office at Boston.

(1)                                              Ex'm'd pr F. Addington Sec'y.

Other pirates came to the island at a later period for plunder—assaulting and wounding the proprietor. During the Revolutionary War there were frequent raids by the British for stock and other products. At the same time British seamen, from the men-of-war anchored in the bay, made it their sporting ground.

John Lyon Gardiner, seventh proprietor, was highly intelligent, and especially fond of antiquarian research. His manuscripts relating to the family and to the island and adjacent places, are invaluable to the historian. He secured the Genevan Bible—printed at London 1599.(2) Also an Indian Bible—printed at Cambridge, Mass., 1663—the first printing office established in America.(3)

The title-page of the Indian Bible is printed in English as follows:

"The Holy Bible containing the old testament and the new. Translated into the Indian language and ordered to be printed by the Commissioners of the United Colonies of New England. At the charge and with the consent of the corporation In England for the propogation of the gospel amongst the Indians of New England—Cambridge, printed by Samuel Green and Marmaduke Johnson MDCLXIII."

The following is the heading over the first chapter of the Old Testament, together with the first verse in Genesis:

*Negonne oosukkuhwhchouk Moses. Ne asweetamuk.*

GENESIS.

1. *Wetke kutchitsik a aytum god kesuk kah olike.*

The following is the commencement of the New Testament, with the first verse in Matthew:

(1) It is said one diamond was carelessly dropped by the officials at Gardiner's Island, which was found after their departure, and is now in the possession of the family of Gardiner Green, of Boston, a descendant of a daughter of John Gardiner, third proprietor. Parties frequently ask permission to dig for Kidd's treasure at the island.—C. C. G. "My father when a young man was sent by his father, and a chart given him to dig up some of Kidd's buried treasures near Montauk Point. They were scared away by the Montauk Indians, and never returned. I copied the chart when a boy, and may have it still."—Letter from Dr. T. W. Colt, Middletown, Ct., Aug. 7, 1883.

(2) Vide Supra, p. 11.

(3) "I received this Indian Bible from Joshua Nonesuch of the Nihoutic tribe in Lyme— by means of Daniel Wankent, this 17th day of May, 1813. It is said to have been presented to the tribe by a Sachem of the Moheags in Norwich, Ct."—Mem. by John Lyon Gardiner, seventh proprietor.

# APPENDIX.

## GARDINER'S ISLAND.

MRS. M. L. GARDINER.

" Where now, it may be ask'd, are all
Those tawny tribes ? From off this beauteous Isle,
By time's rude hand, swept like the sands which
Rolling waves have buried into the deep.  Where
The tall chiefs, who strode like spirits o'er this
Sunny Isle, threading the forest by their magic
Trail, marshalling their hosts, sole monarchs of the
Soil ?
             *       *       *
                  All, all are gone!  Oblivion's
Wave, with waters dark and deep, roll o'er their
Dust, their memories and their names."

This island originally belonged to the jurisdiction of the Montauk Indians, and was purchased from the aboriginal owners by Lion Gardiner, by deed bearing date May 3, 1639, (1) called by them Manchonack ; and from the grantee of the King of England by a grant bearing date March 10, 1640, (2) called by the English Isle of Wight.  It was created a Manor.  On the death of Lion Gardiner he bequeathed (3) his whole estate to his wife, who, at her death, bequeathed (4) the island to her son David—" during his life, and after his decease to his next heire maile begotten by him" and "to be entayled to the first heires maile proceeding from the body," of her late husband and herself, "from time to time forever."  October 5, 1665. David Gardiner procured a grant from Governor Nicoll for a quit-rent of £5 a year.  September 23, 1670, he procured a release from Governor Lovelace for one lamb yearly, if it should be demanded.  November 1, 1683, the General Assembly of New York divided the province into counties and towns, and included the Isle of Wight within the county of Suffolk—the island still retaining its

---

(1) Vide Supra, p. 75, note (a).  Also Vide Supra, p. 51, note (2).   (2) Vide Supra, p. 82, note (1).
(3) Vide Supra, p. 85.   (4) Vide Supra, p. 85.

13

manorial rights and privileges.    September 11, 1686, David Gardiner
procured a grant from Governor Dongan by which the island was
erected into the "Lordship and Manor of Gardiner's Island," for one
lamb yearly in lieu of all services whatsoever. (1)    March 7, 1788,
the State Legislature passed an act attaching the island to the town
of East Hampton in the county of Suffolk, which is its present polit-
ical status.

The locality of the island is north-east of the bay of the same
name, about three miles east of Long Island.    Its greatest length,
including the sand bars at the two extremities, is nearly seven and
a half miles.    Its greatest width slightly exceeds one mile.    The
general outline of the shore is irregular, and portions of the surface
are uneven, with here and there fresh water ponds and patches of
deep forest.    The whole island contains upwards of three thousand
acres of good land.

The first, third and seventh proprietors are the most conspicu-
ously mentioned in history.    A sketch of Lion Gardiner, first
proprietor, occupies this volume.    While John Gardiner, third proprietor, was in possession, Kidd, the notorious pirate, visited the
island at least twice.    At one time he came in the absence of the
proprietor, and requested the proprietor's wife to roast him a pig.
She being afraid to refuse him, cooked it well, which pleased him,
and on his departure he presented her with two small blankets of
gold cloth—a small remnant of one of them still remains with the
relics of the family. (2)    At another time Kidd came, and, in the presence of the proprietor, buried a quantity of gold, silver and precious
stones, enjoining upon him the most solemn pledges of secrecy.
After the arrest of Kidd, the burial of the treasure was made known,
and government officials were dispatched to secure it.    Having taken

---

(1) The fees for these executive grants, under the seal of the province, was a perquisite of the Governors—
to fill their pockets at the expense of the people.—Thompson's His., I., I., I, pp. 139-147.    Gov. Nicoll
gathered a harvest of fees from exacting new title deeds.    Under Gov. Lovelace, his successor, the same
system was more fully developed.—Bancroft's His. of the U. S., II, pp. 320, 321.

(2) I have a small particle of the gold cloth which was clipped off from the remnant and presented to me
by Mrs. Gardiner, widow of the seventh proprietor, at the island, August 9th and 10th, 1855.—C. C. G.

# INDEX.

*Wunanachemookaonk Nashpe.*

MATTHEW.

1. *Uppometuongane a book Jesus Christ wunnaumooauh David wunnaumonuh Abraham.*

The island has been a plantation by itself from its earliest occupancy—continuing, without interruption, in the possession of the descendants of the first purchaser. Prior to the Revolutionary War the proprietors were called, after the custom in England, *Lords* of the Manor, and, for some time later, the *soubriquet* was extended to them by the courtesy of their neighbors.

The usual approach to the island is from the shore of Long Island, at a post-village called "the Springs." There is no harbor on the island—only a boat-house. The mansion fronts to the west, near the shore. The present structure was erected by the sixth proprietor and is upwards of a century old—large, two-story, with wide gables and dormer windows, a deep porch in front, and is shaded by forest trees of venerable and stately appearance. Within this large and hospitable abode there are many relics and priceless heirlooms—fire arms, hunting trophies, paintings, books, documents, plate, and the family coat of arms. The cemetery is located about a half a mile east of the mansion, in which there are not to exceed a score of graves including the several proprietors, from the fourth to the tenth inclusive. The first proprietor was buried at East Hampton,(1) the second at Hartford, (2) the third at New London.(3)

The island is a charming spot. As a plantation it is devoted chiefly to grazing and stock raising. Further than this our subject does not require any particulars.

(1) Vide Supra, p. 86.

(2) The tombstone of David Gardiner, second proprietor, was lost to his descendants for a great many years. He was buried in the rear of the Centre Church, Hartford, Ct., and over his grave was placed a horizontal slab of red sand stone, with an inscription, which in the course of time became partly imbedded in the earth and its whereabouts was not known for at least a century. In 1835 Mr. J. W. Barber of New Haven, discovered the stone and with considerable difficulty, deciphered the inscription, as follows:

"HERE LYETH THE BODY OF MR. DAVID GARDINER OF GARDINER'S ISLAND, DECEASED JVLY 10, 1689, IN THE FIFTY-FOVRTH YEAR OF HIS AGE  WELL, SICK, DEAD, IN ONE HOVRS SPACE.

"ENGRAVE THE REMEMBRANCE OF DEATH ON THINE HEART

WHEN AS THOV DOST SEE HOW SWIFTLY HOVRS DEPART."

(3) Vide Supra, p. 87.

## PROPRIETORS OF GARDINER'S ISLAND.

FIRST: Lion Gardiner died in 1663, and left male issue, aged 64.

SECOND: David Gardiner, only son of Lion. Bequeathed to him as a life estate, by the will of his mother, to be entailed to the first heirs male, from time to time forever. Died in 1689, and left male issue, aged 53.

THIRD: John Gardiner, eldest son of the preceding David. Died in 1738, and left male issue, aged 77.

FOURTH: David Gardiner, eldest son of the preceding John. Died in 1751, and left male issue, aged 60.

FIFTH: John Gardiner, eldest son of the preceding David. Died in 1764, and left male issue, aged 36.

SIXTH: David Gardiner, eldest son of the preceding John. Died in 1774, and left male issue, aged 36.

SEVENTH: John Lyon Gardiner, eldest son of the preceding David. Died in 1816, and left male issue, aged 46.

EIGHTH: David Johnson Gardiner, eldest son of the preceding John Lyon. Died in 1829, unmarried and intestate, aged 25. There being no heir male the island became an inheritance to the next of kin. In common parlance, the entail was broken.

NINTH: John Griswold Gardiner, brother of the preceding David Johnson. Purchased the interests of other heirs and became the owner in fee simple. Died unmarried and intestate in 1861, aged 49.

TENTH: Samuel Buell Gardiner, brother of the preceding David J. and John G. Purchased the interests of other heirs. Died in 1882, aged 67.

ELEVENTH: David J. Gardiner, eldest son of the preceding Samuel Buell. Bequeathed to him by his father, and he sold to his brother J. Lyon Gardiner.

TWELFTH: J. Lyon Gardiner, brother of the preceding David J. Owned by purchase.